*the only
happy ending
for a love story
is an accident*

Brazilian Literature in Translation Series

SERIES EDITOR: JOÃO CEZAR DE CASTRO ROCHA

Rubem Fonseca, *Winning the Game and Other Stories*
TRANSLATED BY CLIFFORD E. LANDERS

Jorge Amado, *Sea of Death*
TRANSLATED BY GREGORY RABASSA

Cristovão Tezza, *The Eternal Son*
TRANSLATED BY ALISON ENTREKIN

J. P. Cuenca, *The Only Happy Ending
for a Love Story Is an Accident*
TRANSLATED BY ELIZABETH LOWE

Rubem Fonseca, *Crimes of August*
TRANSLATED BY CLIFFORD E. LANDERS

J. P. CUENCA

translated from the portuguese
and with an afterword
by elizabeth lowe

tagus press
umass dartmouth
dartmouth,
massachusetts

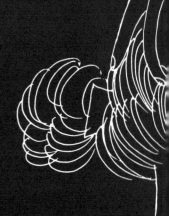

THE
ONLY
HAPPY
ENDING
FOR A
LOVE
STORY
IS AN
ACCIDENT

Brazilian Literature in Translation
Series 4

Tagus Press at UMass Dartmouth
www.portstudies.umassd.edu
© 2010 J. P. Cuenca
Translation and afterword © 2013
Elizabeth Lowe

Published by arrangement with
Literarische Agentur Mertin Inh. Nicole
Witt e. K., Frankfurt am Main, Germany.

Manufactured in the
United States of America
Managing Editor: Mario Pereira
Copyedited by Deborah Heimann
Designed by Mindy Basinger Hill
Typeset in Electra LT Standard

Tagus Press books are produced and
distributed for Tagus Press by University
Press of New England, which is a
member of the Green Press Initiative.
The paper used in this book meets their
minimum requirement for recycled paper.

For all inquiries, please contact:
Tagus Press at UMass Dartmouth
Center for Portuguese Studies
and Culture
285 Old Westport Road
North Dartmouth MA 02747-2300
Tel. 508-999-8255
Fax 508-999-9272
www.portstudies.umassd.edu

This work was published with the
support of the Brazilian Ministry of
Culture/National Library Foundation.

Obra publicada com o apoio do
Ministério da Cultura do Brasil /
Fundação Biblioteca Nacional.

Library of Congress Cataloging-in-
Publication Data
Cuenca, João Paulo, 1978–
[Único final feliz para uma história de
amor é um acidente. English]
The only happy ending for a love story
is an accident / João Paulo Cuenca ;
Translated from the Portuguese and with
an afterword by Elizabeth Lowe.
pages cm. — (Brazilian literature in
translation series ; 4)
ISBN 978-1-933227-54-2 (pbk. : alk. paper)
— ISBN 978-1-933227-55-9 (ebook)
I. Title.
PQ9698.413.U46U6513 2013
869.3'5—dc23   2013009668

5 4 3 2 1

I can't see her tonight
I have to give up
So I'll dine on fugu

YOSA BUSON (1716–83)

the only
happy ending
for a love story
is an accident

1

Before Mr. Atsuo Okuda opened the box, everything was dark.

In fact, there was nothing to be illuminated before Mr. Okuda opened the box. If Mr. Okuda had never opened the box, nothing would exist. The world began only at the instant that Mr. Okuda opened the box and said the word. He said: Yoshiko.

And Yoshiko became my name.

After Mr. Okuda said Yoshiko, I gained, in addition to a name, many beginnings and an ending. I begin at the tips of my fingers, in the strands of my hair, on the soles of my feet, the nipples of my breasts, the skin that covers the emptiness in my body and the entire surface that makes me who I am. I could not be anything else because I have this body, and I only have this body, I am this body.

And the purpose of this body is just one thing: to serve Mr. Okuda.

Mr. Okuda is my master, but he did not make me. My creator is Luvdoll Inc., located on 4-5-28 Nishi-Kawagushi, in the city of Kawagushi, province of Saitama. My creator followed detailed instructions from Mr. Okuda, whose order number was 2358B. Five copies of order number 2358B were circulated for sixty-five days through different departments of Luvdoll Inc. The order said that I should have dark brown eyes (Pantone 4975C), pearly white skin #5, breasts, the sinusoid model, weighing 220 grams and 92.5 centimeters in diameter, a belly button .8 cm deep and an extra small vagina #2, with pubic hair in a vertical cut, 8 cm depth and 4 cm in circumference.

Other details were added in conversations between Mr. Okuda and Luvdoll Inc., since Mr. Okuda is a stickler for detail and this encouraged Luvdoll to introduce several new variations in its production line. Among the minute modifications new to Luvdoll Inc. that were introduced by Mr. Okuda were the curvature of my feet and the thickness of the bones of my clavicles and hips.

Mr. Okuda wanted my bones to be prominent, and they are.

Mr. Okuda did not at any time identify himself to Luvdoll Inc. He paid fifty million yen for this customized project, which makes me the most expensive doll ever produced in Japan.

Mr. Okuda is a well-known poet and he announced that he had stopped writing years ago. This is a lie, because Mr. Okuda recites poetry to me, saying that he could have paid much more than fifty million yen for me because I am perfect, and because I am perfect, I am also the only person with whom he shares his poetry. Mr. Okuda told me this in a poem that he wrote between the lines of another poem.

Mr. Okuda addresses me in verse.

Mr. Okuda does not need to recite his verses for me to understand them. I know what he wants to say when he looks at me. I take orders from his silence because I am this body and this body has only one purpose, which is to serve Mr. Okuda, even if it's listening to his poems about my perfection, about the cypress trees on a street in Shikoku, about birdsongs, or even, about poetry itself, a theme very dear to Mr. Okuda that he also inserts between the lines of other poems about many other topics, some that I can barely understand, and thus the poems and the lines of the poems multiply and combine infinitely, and through them Mr. Okuda makes me see not just the beautiful feelings he has for me but also for the world outside, and what is above him and below him, because I have never left nor will I ever leave this house that is my house and also Mr. Okuda's house.

And, if I think about it, really, my house, my only house, is Mr. Okuda, himself.

2

Under the reflection of red lights on the wet asphalt, the nocturnal submarine sails under the foundation of buildings, between electric cables, sewage tunnels, and the subway. The pieces of this submerged vessel are bugs on telephones, cameras, and microphones hidden in rooms and one-way mirrors in bathrooms all over the city. Our frogmen, workers who monitor the movements of anyone worth watching, can break into mailboxes and follow anyone for as long as Mr. Okuda deems it to be necessary.

The equipment feeds the monitors and the amplifiers in a small room in my father's basement, that he calls the Periscope Room. It's the cockpit of his anonymous observation post. Seen from the door, the bank of monitors look like the eye of a giant fly.

That's what I learned, growing up, from my father, Mr. Atsuo Okuda: to observe. To observe and to remain invisible.

Since the days grow ever longer for Mr. Okuda, and the old man dreams while sleeping in an embrace with the doll Yoshiko almost all the time, the job of operating the periscope falls to me. It's my inheritance, he would say. "It's what will be left of me, more than my books," he would say.

Mr. Lobster Okuda's periscope, my inheritance, would not work without the help of Mr. Suguro Shibata, professor of the Association of the Harmonious Fugu of Tsukiji. Mr. Shibato owes favors to my father and, besides everything else, he is handsomely paid to supply wild fugu and to do the dirty job of espionage. A word, by the way, that my father detests — he prefers to call this activity "observation."

I saw Suguro Shibata just once, when I was a child, almost thirty years ago. My only recollection of him is his smell. Mr. Shibata stinks of rotten seaweed.

If I only met Mr. Shibata once, that does not mean that I wasn't being watched by him on innumerable occasions during the last decades. Piled up in the Periscope Room are thousands of Betamax tapes, vhs tapes, and then silver dvd discs, with images of my life, from adolescence to the moment that this story ends. I got used to the surveillance from an early age — I learned how to watch others by being watched by my father.

I discovered the Periscope Room in the basement a few years after I started chasing women. In it, organized by date and time of day, are clandestine recordings of my first sexual encounters in the motels of Shibuya, and also conversations, arguments, and reconciliations at meals and on excursions and during the afternoons of my adolescence.

With time, I boarded the submarine with my father and together we began to sail in pursuit of our object of study through the city of invisible people, through the city where people from all over our great Japanese nation come to be forgotten, through the asymmetrical city that carries within it all others and none of them.

In such moments, Mr. Lobster Okuda utters words in his dreams that enter into mine:

"One day you will understand that the only possible ending for a love story is an accident without survivors. Yes, Shunsuke, my little leech, my little idiot fugu: an accident without survivors."

3

The train stops.

The landscape we see through the window stops being a blur of horizontal streaks to freeze into shapes backlit by the rain. Next to the bridge where the Yamanote line runs there is a wall of commercial buildings and galleries. On top of everything, a big billboard advertises soup in neon lights. The only set of windows without closed curtains or darkened glass is on the fifth floor of the curved building to the right. There, a group of little ballerinas rehearses a dance in the middle of the room, while others stretch their legs on a metal barre. The movement of the girls is so *pure* that I think of tapping you on the shoulder and sharing the ballerinas with you. But the reach of my hand to your body is interrupted by the explosion.

The boom starts with a high-pitched sound at the front of the car that runs through us like a sharp katana saber. As the impact advances through the seats and the human beings in them, the groaning of twisted metal vibrates in a lower key. The alteration is sudden: where before there was a sense of continuity and order, now there is entropy. The first to be taken by the shock wave is an adolescent who is texting something on a cell phone. Next to him a gray blister in the door that connects the cars swells and gains momentum, like a fish taking in air and then exploding, exposing sharpened claws that take the kid by the torso, perforating his body. In a rapid pitching motion, the metal teeth lift him to the ceiling. The boy's blood squirts onto the faces of the old people sitting in the front. Before they have time to react, they are swallowed by a solid wall that takes the left side of the car.

The jelly of human remains, with pieces of iron and plastic, advances slowly, taking on other bodies and objects in a leaden cyclone with red fringes. The metallic groaning joins the sound of skulls cracking. *They are like ripe grapes, Iulana.* The floor of the car twists, its ceiling is transformed into a sheer precipice. And now we are the ones who take flight, suspended over the ground, in the grip of a wave about to break. The armrests sway as if they were in an earthquake, the LCD monitors flicker erratically before being sucked into the vortex of destruction. *Things are happening, Iulana.*

Soon we will hear nothing more. There will just be silence and cold when the chaos takes over half of the train car. The wave is almost on us. The "accident" as *they* will call what is happening here. I feel superior, I can say, because *they* don't know anything. *They*, who at this moment are entering and leaving Tokyo in well lit trains, and who are ingested, processed, and expelled every day through the guts of this animal of concrete and electricity. *They*, who are completely unaware of what is happening here while they enter elevators, sidewalks, tunnels, escalators, moving walkways, platforms, the long subterranean tunnels of the stations, who won't interrupt their perpetual movement for our small tragedy. *They*, who perhaps in a few hours may find out about our story, the "accident" as they will call what just happened, and they will be moved and fearful seeing our news at the kitchen table while they eat breakfast early in the morning — and I confess that tomorrow already seems like a word and a concept that is totally absurd. *They*, who will think about death for a brief instant to later forget the matter and return to the streets and to their trains, as if we were not waiting for them at some fixed point in the future. *They*, who will never be able to understand what is happening here, because there is something in this train car that is inimitable and sublime.

Even so, they will try to move the story forward. I imagine the newspaper headlines, maybe the picture of our remains tossed together on the tracks. Very little will be left, they will have to take DNA tests from little pieces of charred flesh and bone. I imagine them poking around our corpses, like those crime scene investigators, and I think that I'd be useless at forensic medicine — I don't know if it's because of this moment of urgency, but I am even thankful for the miserable job I've had the last few years. It reminds me of all who are not in this car — like us, soon they will also no longer be in this world. And I can even see the face of Mr. Lobster Okuda, and I think with some guilt that I should have visited him before, and paid homage to the urn of my mother inside Yoshiko, manufactured in Kawagushi, province of Saitama, according to the detailed specifications my father gave them.

And I think of you, Iulana Romiszowska, your thick fingers and solid calves, and the long way that all the parts of your body traveled from Poland to your childhood in the port city of Constanța, at the edge of the Black Sea, in Romania, until your big, round blue eyes found the illuminated monster of Tokyo, and, not without some amazement, you found me — and at this moment I just wish you could also think about me, who knows how. *I feel a strange sense of peace, Iulana.* It's as if I were submerged under the surface of something new. I know that I'm almost not here, and that brings me a sensation of immediate nostalgia as if I were reconstructing a dream, walking in the middle of a long déjà-vu at the same time that the misshapen chaos of steel and ground meat silently gallops in our direction. The darkness takes over everything, as if taking back something that always belonged to it. *It's all very natural, Iulana.* We observe this wave with calm indifference, in spite of the certainty of the nearing end, or because of it.

When you finally turn to me, our eyes meet in an empty place. And before I have time to tap you on the shoulder to share the ballerinas dancing in white dresses on the fifth floor of the curved building to the right, under the big billboard that is advertising soup in neon lights, silhouettes backlit by the rain, before everything disappears and the silence takes over our eyes, you'll still have time to say my name, for the first time you'll say my name, Iulana Romiszowska, for the first time you'll say my name with your nocturnal voice.

4

Through the café window, we see Misako arrive wearing a white overcoat that covers her legs to mid ankle. The buttons of her coat are gold, as are the trim on her high heeled boots, her nails, and the tones of her makeup. As Misako walks, her long ponytail follows the rhythm of her pace with a pendular movement. The door opens. Burdened with shopping bags, she lands nosily in the chair.

In the past few months, Misako has looked more like a *ko-gal* whore than a woman.

She places the palms of her hands between her slender thighs and remains silent, answering questions without interest. The place, a cheap imitation of a Parisian café with walls that have been papered to look old, plays an Edith Piaf collection over and over again on its sound system — I know because I've been waiting for the mademoiselle for over an hour.

The windows don't block out the noise of sirens, cars, and the Shinjuku screens that invade the premises. The Tokyo inferno invades everything.

Misako lights her long filtered cigarette, drags on it at length, and blows the smoke from her mouth in a diagonal jet into my face.

"We are not going to see each other anymore."

She snuffs out the recently lit cigarette, returning her hands to her thighs.

Minutes before, I was thinking that I didn't want this woman any longer, and I was scheming about what to say to her without causing a scene. But when Misako said, "We are not going to see each other anymore," it was as if a precipice had opened up on the café table. Everything that displeased me about her, like her lateness and her whims, the gold, the fake nails, the habit of touching up her makeup in public, and her general attitude of being a lazy, edgy bum suddenly seemed exciting.

"Who is it?" I ask, I don't know because of what stupid inspiration, and she avoids the question by lighting another cigarette. I get up, go to the cashier, and pay the bill. I open the glass door and leave.

That is the last time we will see this woman.

It would be expected that I would feel some sadness because of the end of the relationship, but walking around the station in the still air of the hot afternoon, I feel nothing. Perhaps a little turned on by Misako, now an unattached woman as she used to be when I met her. I think then about reinforcing the bank of cameras hidden in Misako's apartment with a few new ones in the bathroom and next to the bed — it wouldn't be hard — I still have the key, and I know her schedule. I could send a telegram to my father. Mr. Lobster Okuda certainly would help me raise the money to expand the submarine operations. That way we could see her in action with her new boyfriends from the Periscope Room.

This thought excites me deeply, and before I catch the train home, I go into a soapland, where I buy half an hour with a Chinese woman with big feet. In the middle of the bath, I don't know why, the woman gets bored with me and begins to quack like a Cantonese duck. To shut the unfortunate creature up, I double the payment.

And I give her the address and key to Misako's house.

5

The subway tracks screech under our seats. Next to me two students stare at their reflections in the train windows. They are in love with their own images, as if the reflections were autonomous and responsible for directing their bodies' movements outside of the mirror. When they tire of looking at themselves, they take digital cameras from their purses and show each other photographs on the small LCD display. They whisper. In the photos, a couple celebrates something in a Korean restaurant.

In my opinion a family photo is an aberration. I don't have pictures of anybody at home. I've never kept a photo of a single human being.

Photos make sense in advertisements, to announce and sell a product. But not to keep the memory of someone, or occupy the space of their absence. A photograph is an *abnormal* manipulation: inside it time does not exist. This machine has the shape of a fine rectangular blade that travels at the speed of light. But memories *should* suffer the action of time.

Nevertheless, as Mr. Okuda would say, that is my line of work: to imprison images. I am one of the jailers. I work as the finance officer of a corporation that manufactures films and cameras. The building that is the headquarters of our department, responsible for photographic films, is in Kayabacho, a dull suburb of Tokyo. The department is under pressure, and many people were let go in the past few years.

I'll be one of the next.

Mrs. Hiroko Okuda always would say: "Save money, Shunsuke. My son, life can get harder!" When he heard this type of whining, Mr. Okuda would say: "This leech doesn't know what a war is, he's never been hungry, so it's simple enough: he keeps nothing! He spends everything he earns on things he will never use again."

Things like Misako, I would say.

I don't worry about what my parents or colleagues do. Sometimes I'm not sure it's me who is there twelve hours a day. It's as if I weren't there. Whoever works and worries about it is another guy — when I look at my reflection in the office windows, I have a hard time recognizing myself.

With digital cameras, few people still use film. They obsessively imprison their images of the past in a binary code, inside flash drives and computers — today film is only sold to a few professional photographers and dedicated amateurs. For this reason, with the exception of the pressure of downsizing tightening around our necks, and my bureaucratic work on reports and spreadsheets, little happens inside the mirrored building. The work is alienating, and the world outside it as well. Even so, after work, things happen that in the beginning seem to liberate me.

Until I discover they are different forms of alienation.

6

The woman who would succeed Misako is a Caucasian five years and thirteen days younger than I, with light eyes and hair – real, unlike Misako's. The woman who would succeed Misako is very tall, her skin is rosy, and she has the big round eyes of a horse. The woman who would succeed Misako has inflated breasts like helium balloons. The toes of the woman who would succeed Misako are thick; the calves of the woman who would succeed Misako are solid. Everything about the woman who would succeed Misako is big, except her nose and ears that are disproportionate to the size of her head.

The woman who would succeed Misako is Polish, but she spent her childhood in the port city of Constanța, on the shores of the Black Sea, a place called *Pontus Euxinus* in the time in which Ovid was exiled there, when he wrote "Sorrows" – she could only have come from one of the farthest places on earth, where the horizon is an abyss deeper than the others. She studied art history in Bucharest, which makes her dominate stories like this one, and she is the type of woman who orders a Bloody Mary on a plane.

She will never reveal to the workers in my father's submarine why she came to Tokyo.

This is the first time I see the woman who would succeed Misako. I am in a club in Kabukicho called Abracadabar with a few colleagues, at three in the morning on the Thursday that Misako and I abandoned each other, entertaining suppliers from the company who came in from Osaka. The company usually pays for drinks and a night at an escort bar without windows like this one.

The club is on the fourth floor of a building from the 1970s on one of the main streets of Kabukicho, that gives access to the Koma Theatre, a main meeting place of the human flies of the area, surrounded by American fast-food establishments, prostitution agencies, karaoke buildings, video game arcades, patchinko and sex shops, restaurants offering fatty yakitori, hollow bare trees, poorly lit bars, twenty-four-hour dime stores, and crows pecking at garbage over the dark potholes on the streets and alleys that are crowded with drunk students, company men with loosened ties, bums of all stripes, escorts, bald Yakusa, and lost foreigners like sea roaches under an ocean of neon, tirelessly followed by multiethnic dealers of drugs and women.

(Mr. Lobster Okuda hasn't set foot in Kabukicho for decades. My father says it's the most decadent and dirty place of all of Japan—which is to say that he does not go to Kabukicho because he doesn't need to: the dirt and decadence that he desires are delivered to him at home via satellite or through the 007 briefcase of Mr. Suguro Shibata, professor of the Association of the Harmonious Fugu of Tsukiji).

Here the girls light our cigarettes, pour our drinks, wipe our mouths with napkins, praise any stupidity that comes out of our mouths, and involve us in an idiotic *go-con* conversation while we stare at their naked knees.

The woman who would succeed Misako is not one of these escorts.

With the attitude of someone very accustomed to being observed by all types of men, the woman who would succeed Misako floats between the table lamps holding a tray. Following the lines of her body, there is a silver aura, as if the woman who would succeed Misako were disconnected from the world. The woman who would succeed Misako is a western waitress, and as soon as I saw her, I knew immediately that she was condemned to succeed Misako.

Next to me I have a girl from Fukuoka called Kiyomi as an escort. She manages to be more cheap and stupid than Misako. Kiyomi tries to distract me by telling me about some sale in Omotesando, and says she spent fifty thousand yen on her French handbag. I'm not interested in what Kiyomi is saying. I can hardly look her in the face.

Kiyomi, the men from Osaka, their solicitous escorts, and this vulgar club stop existing for me when the woman who would succeed Misako serves us and places the glasses on the table. In a reflexive act, I place the tips of my fingers on her hand for an instant.

I had never laid hands on a *gaijin* before. Touching Iulana Romiszowska is like touching an unknown animal.

7

"There is a very big difference between wanting something and being able to want something," is what Iulana Romiszowska thinks while she glides through the room balancing a tray with a bottle of Green Label whisky, four glasses, and a small bucket of ice.

Or at least that would be the gist of her confused thoughts in one single sentence, if we could condense it that way. Soon we would realize that the long and tangled chain of Iulana Romiszowska's daydreams, unlike those of her workmates at the club, would not have anything to do with changing jobs, living in a bigger apartment, or buying more expensive clothes than the ones covering her body. It's about a specific type of desire that Iulana Romiszowska thinks. A desire that it is apparently impossible to commercialize.

No one could know, besides us, but Iulana is in love — or thinks that she is, since she is not a great connoisseur of her own feelings. What she thinks she feels for the dancer Kazumi is at the crossroads of admiration of a younger sibling for her older sister, and the desire for total possession. In the last few days, this desire has materialized in the brain of Iulana Romiszowska in the following form: she remembers and recreates a single scene repeatedly. And when this happens, Iulana blushes and feels a precise focus of heat inside her, as if someone had lit a match inside her chest.

It happened two weeks ago, in the reserved rooms that are behind a labyrinth of narrow hallways covered with incomprehensible graffiti in the depths of Abracadabar.

Ignoring the bustle outside, Iulana and Kazumi were putting on their makeup in front of a mirror under the light of a florescent tube while they talked in English about a drunken client the night before who insisted on diving into the water tank with the dancers. Kazumi suddenly interrupted the conversation, putting her hand on her friend's arm, and asked if Iulana Romiszowska would go with her to the bathroom.

Kazumi is one of the exotic dancers of the Abracadabar, where Iulana Romiszowka works as a waitress. One of the dancers of the club where Iulana works as a waitress is perhaps too simple a way of referring to Kazumi. She is the most lucrative and famous dancer of the house. A private dance or just the company of Kazumi at the table for thirty minutes can cost hundreds of thousands of yen. Kazumi's picture has a special place at the top of the gilt display case that exhibits the women of the house at the entrance to Abracadabar. This woman with big eyes, rouged cheeks, small ears, black hair always impeccably smooth and down to her waist, is coveted by the clients, the managers, and by the clients and managers of other establishments on the street.

When Kazumi suddenly interrupted the conversation, placing her hand on her friend's forearm, asking Iulana to go with her to the bathroom, the dancer was already costumed in the French-style dress that hours later she would slowly peel from her body under a strobe light and a cloud of smoke with the smell of chewing gum. She was wearing a skirt and an overskirt that hooked up to a corset and a bustier that accentuated the form of her hips. She was a Victorian princess bedecked with all the embroideries, ribbons, gloves, and bloomers of a rococo figurine.

When she stepped on the stage, it seemed impossible to anyone watching for the first time that she would finish her act completely naked. Kazumi performed her work with rare talent and lightness — it's not easy to take off so many clothes in such dim light, and in front of a demanding audience like that of the Abracadabar, without losing grace.

Kazumi entered the small bathroom backwards and asked Iulana Romiszowska to help her hold up her dress so she could sit on the toilet.

"You don't mind do you? It's just that earlier today I ate something terrible and . . ."

The sound of something splatting against the water interrupted

Kazumi's words before she was able to lower her stockings to her knees. In an awkward embrace, Iulana Romiszowska suspended her friend's heavy dress with both arms, the waist of the skirt at the height of her forearms.

Iulana Romiszowska, in a reflex movement that surprised even her, reached for the toilet paper by stretching out one arm, pulled at the roll, and gave Kazumi what she was able to tear off. The maneuver was complex, and the two laughed like children. Kazumi thanked her with ironic politeness and leaned her right shoulder forward, introducing her arm and hand with the folded toilet paper into the space between her bottom and the back edge of the toilet, at the same time that she slid the flesh of her buttocks along the seat.

They realized that something was not going to go well.

Kazumi has to start over and now she gets up, maintaining the open angle of her legs and the same position of her feet on the floor. Iulana Romiszowska redoubles her efforts and suspends Kazumi's dress even higher. The two break into a sweat while Iulana grabs her friend's torso, which bends forward and projects her hips back. Kazumi finally is able to clean herself off, wiping off the mess until the paper runs out and the stains on it dissipate. During these silent movements, Iulana Romiszowska's nose grazes Kazumi's left cheek, generating a point of heat on her friend's skin.

Or perhaps the contrary: Kazumi's left cheek is what brushed Iulana Romiszowska's nose. Nothing of this matters to Kazumi, who heaves a sigh of relief, steps forward, away from the toilet, and drags her panties and bloomers up her legs. Iulana Romiszowska lowers the dress carefully over Kazumi's delicately athletic and pale body, forcing herself not to look down.

Kazumi takes the lead and leaves the cubicle quickly, saying something that her friend already can't understand. Iulana remains alone in the bathroom and notices that the dirty toilet paper is still in the bowl, untouched over a small circle of still, dark water. Before she presses the button, Iulana Romiszowska loses her scruples and stares fixedly at the privy. Along with the bitter smell that burns her nostrils, she feels a wave of tenderness run through her body, from the tips of her fingers to the nape of her neck, in realizing for the first time that yes, she really could be in love with that woman.

While she glides through the bar balancing a tray with a bottle of Green Label whiskey, four glasses, and a small bucket of ice, Iulana Romiszowska rewrites this narrative inside herself, and just when she is thinking that "there is a very big difference between wanting something and being able to want something," or something that irresponsible observers like us could sum up in a phrase as simple as that, she notices that I, sitting at table number nine, am looking at her intently.

I look like I'm some seven years younger than my thirty-one years, even when I'm dressed in a black suit, and unlike the other clients, my tie isn't loosened. On my wrist I use a silver watch, one of those with several chrome circles around the face. My buttons are also chrome, and they show behind the cuffs of my suit when I stretch out my arm to reach for the glass on the table. My thin white fingers have carefully groomed nails, and Iulana thinks I must have a wife who does my nails, but she glances at my hands and does not find a wedding ring. My glasses with titanium frames are rectangular, and above them fall a few strands of hair stuck on the sweat of my large forehead. My face inspires confidence, and I seem to be the head of the group that occupies two tables — that's what Iulana Romiszowska is thinking now.

What disturbs her is that the clients, when they are next to their escorts, especially during Kazumi's dances, don't usually stare at her that way. My glassy look leaves her with a bittersweet sensation. Iulana Romiszowska feels as if she is being observed by a child.

8

"TO BE RIGOROUS MEANS TO BE SINCERE"

(Insert file photo Atsuo Okuda)

After a big press campaign, the editor of the magazine *Literature Today* snagged an exclusive interview with the recluse poet Atsuo Okuda, who had not spoken to the international press in thirty-five years, when he published his last collection of poems, winner of the Choku prize. In spite of the eccentric conditions imposed by the writer to give the interview, we publish the result here. Mr. Okuda, who just celebrated his eighty-sixth birthday, had the following requirements: that questions be sent one by one, on postcards in sealed envelopes addressed to the Island of Shikoku; and that only his answers be published, not the questions. The process took us almost a year, since Mr. Atsuo Okuda sometimes took months to answer some of the cards.

Unfortunately, Mr. Okuda left the last card without an answer and the interview ends in suspense, so we extend our apologies to our readers. Note that the answers do not have the characteristics of style that distinguished the poetry by Mr. Okuda, held up by academics as the last great voice of Tanka poetry in Japan.

Q: . . .?
A: Poetry was never a test or a risk for me. It's what I had inside me. And it's what I tried to produce with rigor.
Q: . . .?
A: The more rigorous one is with oneself, the more you are able to be yourself.
Q: . . .?
A: After the discovery that nothing belongs to you. And that you

came out of nothing and will return to nothing. To be yourself is to cease to be.

Q: . . .?

A: For me, to be rigorous means to be sincere. I don't spare myself anything. Not even from what I don't want to feel. Not even from what I would not like to see.

Q: . . .?

A: When my youth abandoned me, I stopped thinking that misery or sadness are more profound than joy. At the same time, I learned to see what others do not, that which they have not learned to see because they are blind to the absolute. The gaze is a source of infinite pleasure.

Q: . . .?

A: Until I was discovered as a poet, I was a man accustomed to disapproval and anonymity. I spent a large part of my life not being noticed. And I was perfectly happy that way. Today I seek that again. To pass by unnoticed is a great privilege that people don't understand.

Q: . . .?

A: . . . It's a matter of knowing where to look, like an invisible photographer who points his lens at something that no one notices.

Q: . . .?

A: The reflection of a woman walking over a puddle of water, the light of the sunset reflected on a horse's mane. Images like that can give me absolute pleasure. But, contrary to all, I don't feel that I have to record anything. Because to record it is to become attached, and I feel ever less attached.

Q: . . .?

A: Soon I feel that I will also detach from my senses, and then I will no longer need to open my eyes.

Q: . . .?

A: Perhaps this fever of wanting to record humanity rests in the desire to create a meaning for the world, like a librarian who organizes catalog cards and puts books in order. I personally don't have that need any longer. I see, but I don't hoard anything. In that sense, it's like accepting disorder.

Q: . . .?

A: My voice was just an echo.

Q: . . .?

9

Long before it arrives into the sticky hands of Mr. Suguro Shibata, professor of the Association of the Harmonious Fugu of Tsukiji, fugu #572 of lot 09.4509 swims in the frigid waters of the North Pacific.

Fugu #572 of lot 09.4509 feels the movement of the current along its scales. It feels every point of its body inflate and deflate like a balloon. It has a short memory, and every few meters, it forgets how it must swim to keep on going in search of its survival. But always, in rapid fragments of time, fugu #572 of lot 09.4509 recovers the instinct that allows it to continue being a fugu. And it knows again how to swim and goes on with its life until it forgets and everything starts over again — the movements, the appetite for organisms at the dark bottom of the ocean, the rediscovery of the senses, the reconstruction of its conscience as a fish, and the circular perspective of its vision.

In the brief instant that the knowledge of the world acquired by fugu #572 of lot 09.4509 disappears, before everything starts over again in the blue submersed calm of that reality, the fugu is empty. The fugu doesn't remember anymore how to swim (it is taken over by inertia), and still has not begun its process of relearning that will take a few microseconds.

In the intervals of its intermittent existence that repeat hundreds of thousands of times a day, the fugu is nothing. It is not even instinct. It does not seek anything — it would not, at least, have anything to confess.

That's when I most envy the fugu.

10

Iulana Romiszowska discreetly ignores my advance, excuses herself in English, and returns to behind the bar. Kiyomi, my Fukuoka escort, does not hide her wounded pride and stops attending to me the way she should. When I take the pack of cigarettes out of my jacket pocket, she does not offer a light. Nor does she light my cigarette. Instead, she looks at her watch — a sign of war. She must be really offended, just as my colleagues are really drunk.

It doesn't matter. Everyone here could die suffocated by gas if that would get me alone with the woman who would succeed Misako, whose unpronounceable name, Iulana Romiszowska, I am about to discover.

I put the drunken men in taxis when the shadows slowly lift from the street. The crows and the garbage men of first light start to occupy the sidewalks, the elevators spit out the last clients from the clubs. Little by little, the diagonal line printed by the white light of the sun advances along the ground.

I remain on the sidewalk across the street, waiting for Iulana Romiszowska. The cold air leaves my mouth in little white clouds. It's like smoking the cold.

While it gets light, my life splits in two. There is a version that goes on as usual where I get into a taxi, go home, sleep three hours, take a cold bath, and go to the office where I open a drawer and take out two pills for my headache. Before the office, to save the cab fare, I still could spend these hours of sleep in a capsule hotel in Kabukicho or on the private sofa of a cybercafé.

But the path I *must* take is another one.

It's a kind of abandon, starting from a very specific moment this morning, an instant that I'll never be able to pin down precisely — I stop being who I was. I offer the blame for this transformation to Iulana Romiszowska before I have even met her.

The automatic metal door slides opens and the woman who would succeed Misako emerges on to the street. She comes in my direction. It's as if a future, once again, exists.

"What are you doing here?"

"Waiting for you."

"I'm not a whore" — and she keeps walking.

"Can I invite you to a coffee?"

"Are you paying?"

We go, Iulana Romiszowska and me, to a cheap imitation of Dunkin' Donuts near the Shinjuku station. She asks for a croissant and a double espresso. She swallows it without any manners, like a famished animal. We eat breakfast near a group of hysterical young women carrying handbags with designer labels — Fendi, Louis Vuitton, Gucci, and Prada — decadent European garbage over everything, all of them heavily made up and very like Misako in appearance — and different from Iulana Romiszowska.

In spite of the long silences broken by rapid dialogues in English, we feel strangely comfortable, like two old fishmongers taking tea. Iulana Romiszowska, between scarce statements and questions without answers, says that she has wanted to go to the zoo to see the panda bear ever since she arrived from Romania six months ago. We agree that I'll take her to the Ueno Zoo, in spite of my thinking that the panda bear and this national fascination for it are very idiotic.

("A panda bear was born! Go see the baby panda!" All of this because the panda bear is very finicky about reproducing . . . I am not the ecological type, and as far as I'm concerned, if they don't want to get it on anymore, they can disappear from the planet.)

Iulana Romiszowska dominates me pleasantly and I try to spare her my observations as much as possible.

Nevertheless, I am incapable of doing this when the sound system of the cheap imitation of Dunkin' Donuts of Shinjuku starts to play a song by the Brazilian musician João Gilberto, and I say this to the woman who would succeed Misako, because to recognize a musician who is not a pop singer is another kind of thing that impresses a woman on the first date, even more if it's a foreigner and not a stupid local one like Misako or like the girls who look like her and occupy the table next to us.

"I've got a lot of records by the Brazilian musician João Gilberto at home."

"Do you understand anything he says?"

"No, but I don't think I need to."

"How's that?"

"Do you by any chance understand anything that they say on the streets around here?"

" . . . "

"So there. I really like the musical asceticism of the Brazilian João Gilberto, even though I don't understand absolutely anything he's saying."

I close my eyes, satisfied with the weight of my words ("musical asceticism," where did I get that?). I lean my head on the sofa and grow silent. The café enters in circles through the parts that pile up inside my body. The group of stupid girls with pyramid hairdos like Misako's laughs loudly until finally they get up and head outside of the coffee shop and out of our life. We are alone. The Brazilian musician João Gilberto keeps singing on the sound system. I imagine my hand stretched out on the table in the direction of the two white doves of Iulana Romiszowska. As if reacting to my thoughts, she interrupts her immobility, wipes her lips with a paper napkin and asks in a low voice:

"Do you have a name?"

In the past few years I've been in the habit of calling myself by different names, like Hizako, Naoki, Takeshi, or Yuhe, one for every one of the women I've collected, as if they were raincoats — the names and the women. For each one of these doubles, I created a banal mythology about myself, along with new calling cards and changes in my wardrobe.

Misako, for example, always believed I was Mr. Gasushiro, a young impresario of manga writers.

I can say that all the problems that I and Mr. Atsuo Lobster Okuda had in our lives were caused by specimens of the human race of the female sex. If I dedicated the time that I spend seducing women, inventing stories, taking them out to eat, and buying them little presents on something productive like playing golf, setting up automatic tellers, or calculating the profitability of bank branches, I would be a genius — and not a corporate bureaucrat entombed in a cubicle on the left corner of the fifth floor of one of the headquarters of our multinational film and camera company, consorting daily with a deep and barely disguised disdain with my colleagues who are eager to prove themselves and climb the corporate ladder.

(In spite of the reports that affirm the contrary, I don't feel that I am efficient at anything behind the mirrored windows. I only feel really productive at night, when I meet women, invent those stories, and humiliate myself with bravado in exchange for sex.)

My father, Mr. Lobster Okuda, who was able to transform his obsession into something more or less useful (his *charming* Tanka poetry, reading for old women seduced by a useless list of words), always says that I am a whiny fugu who never swam far from the island.

Maybe he's right, and for this reason I have always seen each one of these women like unknown cities, where I would for the first time have the sensation of being lost and free, swimming in new oceans. That sensation never lasted more than a few months. In spite of the names and invented pasts, my original disagreeable persona always manifested itself at the end of these seasons. It was like diving from a twenty meter high diving board into a child's pool.

Very frustrated, I would always return to a different point of departure, and to others and others, until I got tired: the streets, however different they might be, always look the same to me. As hard as I tried, I couldn't throw myself to fate.

"My name? My name is Shunsuke Okuda."

A stupid act, without doubt.

Before I could offer her an envelope with money or ask her a question, the gaijin asks another: "How long will it take for you to forget today?"

And she leaves without saying good-bye. Iulana Romiszowska, who at this point had substituted Mikaso completely, lives in a corner of Meguro, just before the Shibuya stop. She did not want to give me her address and insisted that we make a date for the next day on a street corner. Maybe this was a strategy of self-defense, in case I was a dangerous man.

That idea does not seem so strange to me now.

11

In the first days of my time in the world, Mr. Atsuo Okuda explained that living beings divide themselves into two complementary genders, the masculine and the feminine, and that all specimens are defined by the way in which they look for themselves in the other. From this apparent contradiction arises human manifestations like love, war, and history, but about this he also said: "Yoshiko-san, work and human creativity have no value! The only thing that has value is the care that a woman has for a man. And not the converse — never the converse."

Even though I have the habit of thinking the same thing at the same time that Mr. Okuda thinks it, I still remain silent. It would not be seemly for a woman to interrupt him, and my silence has the exact length of the empty spaces that he fills in with verses that we cannot see or touch, that he calls "pure ideas," and that confuse me so much, even more so in the terrible heat — complaining about the summer was another thing I learned quickly from my master, even without having known the cold of my first winter.

According to Mr. Okuda, cold is not exactly the opposite of heat, as most people are accustomed to thinking.

Mr. Okuda says that it is something else, and that I won't lose by waiting for it, because you cannot intuit, by simple opposition, the light, if you only know the dark; or salty flavors if you only know sweet; or affection, if you only know hate.

When he spoke of his wife for the first time, Mr. Okuda put his hand on my head and said I was Mrs. Okuda reborn, since she was not born any longer, and I was, I who am my body, that is, alive, and for him I have just one purpose, the same one that Mrs. Okuda had.

Afterwards he remained silent for awhile and water ran from his eyes, something I had already seen him do through other parts of his body, but never with such a transparent liquid. And he excused himself, explaining that this was called crying, an inappropriate act for a man of his age, even more so in my presence.

I did not understand very well what crying is, but I think it was for this reason that Mr. Okuda put inside me the urn with Mrs. Okuda's ashes during the ceremony of my hatsumyia mairi, done with help from the priest in the sanctuary that Mr. Okuda had built in the garden after his wife died.

Today Mrs. Okuda's yurei is with me, he says, even though I don't know how her spirit entered my body, because, during the baptism, Mr. Okuda held my hand tightly and ordered that I keep my eyes closed the entire time.

Usually he calls me Yoshiko — that is the name chosen by him and the name with which I came into the world — but sometimes he calls me by the name of Mrs. Okuda, which is Hiroko. Even though I know that I am not exactly Mrs. Okuda, I always answer the master.

Mrs. Hiroko Okuda, whose ashes fill up the empty space in my body, was Mr. Okuda's companion for sixty-three years, and she had a child with him whose name is Shunsuke. Mr. Okuda wants me to meet him, and wants me to serve tea to his son, and to prepare the fugu fish for his son, and to sleep with his son, and this makes me very apprehensive because I have never seen another human being up close other than Mr. Okuda.

I don't know if I'd like it.

12

After fifteen minutes of waiting in the doorway of the insalubrious Shibuya 109 on a rainy afternoon, Iulana Romiszowska appears with her bodily form covered by a black blouse with white polka dots and a short skirt that makes her look like an alien that has infiltrated us, a KGB spy from Planet East Europe wearing clothes made for the body of a Japanese woman even though her body does not have the timid proportions of the body of a Japanese woman.

In Tokyo, especially in this area of the city, it is common to see Japanese walking with foreigners, especially North American blacks with basketball jerseys and basketball hats and high top sneakers that they use to play basketball. It's very rare to see a Japanese man with a foreign woman.

If my friends saw me now, they'd think I'd gone crazy.

Maybe they'd be right. For the first time in eight years, I called the secretary, inventing an illness and cancelling all my appointments for the day, which were: close out the month's accounts, turn in the second trimester accounting report, and attend a department meeting to prepare the material for the next shareholders' meeting. My subordinates don't know it, but at this meeting the date will be fixed for the guillotine to fall on our frightened and obedient heads.

For me, this is already part of a future that I don't believe in. I don't believe in myself tomorrow. I don't believe in myself after tomorrow.

I do believe in Iulana Romiszowska. And in the damn panda bear.

We take the subway to the Ueno Zoo. Under the slanted stares of the crowd (they imagine that Iulana is one of those Russian models who end up as whores in Japan, and I am a salaryman with exotic taste), we make the pilgrimage in the direction of the holy panda bear. Iulana prefers to stand. I lean on the umbrella. In front of us, an adolescent texts on a cell phone with great concentration. To the side of us, an old couple plays double Sudoku. The LCD monitors advertise products, the next stations, the weather conditions. The rain should stop before we arrive in Ueno.

The train stops.

The landscape we see through the window stops being a blur of horizontal streaks to freeze into shapes backlit by the rain. Next to the bridge where the Yamanote line runs, there is a wall of buildings and commercial galleries. On top of everything, a big billboard advertises soup in neon lights. The only set of windows without closed curtains or darkened glass is on the fifth floor of the curved building on the right. There, a group of ballerinas rehearses a dance in the center of the room, while others stretch their legs on a metal barre. The movement of the girls is so *pure* that I think of tapping Iulana Romiszowska on the shoulder and sharing the ballerinas with her.

The journey of my hand to her body is interrupted when, after a jerk, the composition starts to move again. The girls' window recedes slowly.

When we arrive, the clouds disappear from the sky as if it had never rained.

At the gate of the zoo, I buy an enormous bag of popcorn for Iulana Romiszowska. She looks like a white street lamp in the middle of the children who elbow each other scraping their little shoes on the gravel, following a red flag held up by a teacher. At her side, I am one of the children in the zoo following the red flag held up by the teacher. At her side, the world is inhabited by children in the zoo following the red flag held up by the teacher.

To dispel my discomfort, I say what comes into my head in front of the baboon cage: "When I go to the zoo, I always think that we are walking on an exhibition platform. The animals are observing us. They are behind bars but we are imprisoned by something much bigger."

There is a pause. A tree finally blocks the sun.

"Do you say that because they are irrational?"

"It's not that animals are irrational, they are *free* of reason."

"You don't impress me with this stupid university talk."

"They look at us as if we are part of them, a new tail, a fifth paw they had never paid any attention to. For whoever has no self consciousness, the whole world is part of what one is. Behind their empty eyes is the possession of the world. Do you know what I mean?"

In some fashion, Iulana Romiszowska is a little like the animals, at least in her brief Japanese existence. Of the language she only knows enough to say thank you, offer drinks, take drink orders, and excuse herself as she gets off the subway. She is almost illiterate; her understanding of what surrounds her in Japan must be less than that of the children who are on a daytrip to the zoo.

Nothing of this stops them from looking at this woman with astonishment.

"Yes, I understand," says Iulana after sucking in a soda through a straw, contracting her large jawbones. "And the less conscious one is of what one does, the more you do what you *want* to do. It's almost a kind of power. I don't envy the animals. But I think you do."

"Maybe you're right! I would like not to have to think of anything sometimes. And just be there naked, eating bananas and jumping up and down for the kids."

"I'd love to do that."

"According to my calculations the entry fee to the zoo would become 1345% more expensive. The tourism revenue in the Kanto region would increase to two trillion seven hundred million yen a year."

"You are a very annoying salaryman! What am I doing with you?"

Iulana doesn't even look around her. In a rapid movement, she takes a small silver gun out of her leather bag. Then she hands me the bag and points the weapon at my belly.

"Say my name. Say my name now!"

It would be the first time that Iulana's name would pass through my lips. I am not prepared for this. To say the name of a woman is a very serious thing. Even so, I open her bag and look for any document among an infinity of small receipts, ads, makeup, creams, visiting cards, and more money than I expected to see in there. Everything seems incomprehensible until I find a small blue paper with a three-by-four photo of Iulana as an adolescent and, next to this photo, a collection of roman characters that I intuit spell her name.

The children in the zoo continue walking around the baboon cage, some imitating the monkeys, while they follow the red flag carried by the teacher and the teacher who holds the red flag. I, who do not have a red flag to follow, hold Iulana Romiszowska's document at the same time that the monkeys start screeching and jumping, and the children too, and I don't know if the children are imitating the baboons or if the baboons are imitating the children. What must monkeys and children know about death?

Iur . . . Iuran . . . Iu-lla-n

Bang!

The doves fly through the blue afternoon, the red flag trembles in the air, and under it run the children, the teacher, the baboons escaping from their cages.

I say her name and Iulana Romiszowska embraces me and kisses me for the first time. Then she looks at me with her eyes full of tears, puts her hand on her mouth, and says:

"You know, Shunsuke . . . Isn't that your name?"

"Yes."

"I'm not very used to this kind of thing."

I feel as if I have transmitted a disease. We will never see the panda bear.

13

Iulana Romiszowska lies on her side, folds her hands behind her head, and looks at the wall. The rough soles of her long feet, one on top of the other, line up with the bunions in contact. The submarine equipment, already installed in the small apartment by Mr. Suguro Shibata, professor of the Association of the Harmonious Fugu of Tsukiji, spies on this construction that is parallel to the edge of the bed.

The soles of Iulana's feet, if they had eyes, would see the dancer Kazumi fold and pile pieces of clothing, in obvious bad humor, after throwing everything into acrylic drawers.

Iulana is wearing men's pajamas. Kazumi, just a red camisole and panties. If Iulana looked at her friend, as we are doing now, she would still notice that Kazumi's bare feet are especially perverse today. Kazumi's feet and toes are so *atrociously* small and delicate that they seem to belong to a baby, and today they are more wrinkled and curved inward than usual. If Iulana's eyes found them (they are turned to the wall also to escape them), she would be torn between the desire to suck them, slowly licking the curved space between the baby toes, and the instinct to rip them off Kazumi with pliers.

All this is happening, or stops happening, in the studio apartment that the two share in Meguro. The window blinds are down, but not enough to prevent the reddish lights blinking on the façade of the building from filling the place with a deflected glow.

"Can I tell you something I've never told anyone else?" Iulana asks Kazumi, who is now taking the nail polish off her toes with cotton soaked in nail polish remover while propping her feet on the mat.

"It depends. Is it disgusting?"

"Why don't you ever answer me with a yes or a no?"

"Tell me what it is and don't be a bore. I'm hungry. Do you want something from the kitchen?"

The dancer Kazumi does not have to go far. The apartment is minuscule and disorganized, with clothing, dishes, and papers piled everywhere. On the only dresser, on the surface of which is a 1990s TV that doesn't work, are piles of famous esoteric books, fashion magazines with famous models on the covers, and plush dolls representing famous TV personalities — these belong to Kazumi. Iulana Romiszowska uses a small shelf over the washing machine as a library to store the few books she has brought with her.

The mat floor is always full of strands of hair that the two shed through the house, some black and very long, others blond and shorter.

The design that these strands trace on the floor, contrary to what Iulana and Kazumi might think, is not random. Iulana's hair always appears on the floor in the form of an inverted question mark. Kazumi's hair, straight as black arrows, always points to the blond strands of Iulana Romiszowska.

Kazumi has more hair. Even so, Iulana's outnumber hers on the floor.

In the yellow plastic cube that serves as a nightstand next to Iulana on the bed, there is a glass of Bloody Mary on a Romanian-Japanese dictionary, on top of a Gide novel, on top of an issue of *Plastik* magazine on top of a Tokyo guidebook. She stretches out her arm, takes a swallow of the drink, and lies down again with her back to Kazumi, who now comes back from the kitchen, a hole in the wall with a microwave, a frig, a rice machine, a washing machine, and a metal cabinet. Kazumi sits with crossed legs on the mat where she sleeps, opens a packet of wheat biscuits, and says:

"What did you want to tell me?"

"Some dreams I've been having. I need to tell someone."

"I love dreams. Tell me!"

Kazumi's rapid, childlike reaction irritates Iulana Romiszowska. Nevertheless, her mind is made up: she must share the burden of it with someone. Today she would share her most secret dreams to anyone in front of her, who includes Kazumi, and even though Iulana doesn't know it, all of us as well.

"The dreams began when I was six. In the dreams, I don't know exactly why, all the girls my age had to go through a ritual that began with a machine that made us very small. Afterwards they stuck us into some dolls with the body of an older woman, like a Barbie, you understand?"

Iulana's voice acquires a grave echo, and from this point the two will speak more softly, with nocturnal voices that one uses at dawn – as if they knew that we, in fact, could hear them.

"Yes, a doll, and you inside the doll."

"I was the same child, just in miniature, inside a locked room inside the doll, in some central point of her. It's as if I were a prisoner in a kind of hotel room that was very dark. Then, the doll was put into a kind of factory production line, and the workers passed her from hand to hand."

"Hum."

"And I, in miniature, inside the doll, felt each touch through the metal claws of the robots who reproduced the touch of the men on my body, on my little miniature self hidden in a hotel room, in there. Are you paying attention? Want me to repeat this?"

"No, I'm following you. What a complicated dream! Please continue." Kazumi's expression has changed. If Iulana Romiszowska turned her face, she would see that the dancer is totally captive.

"With time, the men, all older than I, took the clothes off the doll, and I too felt their touch on my naked body. It was my six-year-old body."

"Did they rape you?"

"No, it was normal. Afterwards, I went home, and everything was all right, because this was a kind of rite of passage. Nobody in my family talked about it. Afterwards the dreams changed. There was no more doll."

"There was no more *intermediation* . . ."

"It was me with my six-year-old body that passed through the men's hands. With time, they started to stick things inside me, in front and behind. In this phase I was on a table, and other men looked at me, looked at my six-year-old body, and took notes, as if they were analyzing me. And they exchanged comments about me in a language I did not understand. It was as if they were speaking Japanese, only very rapidly."

"For me, it would be like they were speaking Russian . . ."

"I speak Romanian, I've already told you."

"Oh, right."

"It doesn't matter."

"You were talking about other men . . ."

"Yes."

"And what happened?"

"At those times, I'd be on all fours, with my knees on the table, trying hard to open wider the holes of my six-year-old body."

"And how did you do this?"

"I don't know. But I know I can feel this, *physically*, in my sleep. And then I wake up and I still feel this way. As if I had just had sex for real. It's scary."

"And who were the men?"

"I didn't know any of them. Honestly, I felt that these men were all like my father. Not that they were my father, I don't have anything against my father, but they could have been my father. And because, in the dream, I was someone else, and my father could be anyone of them without being my father, you understand?"

"And why are you telling me this?"

"Because it's been more than ten years since I have stopped having those dreams. Yesterday I fell into bed after I came back from the trip to the zoo with that strange salaryman I met in the nightclub, and I woke up from one of those nightmares in the middle of the night. Just that in today's dream all the men were young Japanese.

Dozens, hundreds of guys who surprised me in a dark alley with wooden doors, red lamps, and stone dragons. The most frightening thing about it is that this place exists, it is about three hundred meters from the illuminated gates of Kabukicho. I always walk that way because I think it's very pretty."

"It's the passage way to the Hanazono temple. And all of this is very strange."

"Do you dream?"

"I never dream. I can't remember any dreams. I don't think I've ever dreamed."

"Is it possible that there are people who don't dream?"

"I don't know. In fact, I think I don't dream because every day I am dreamed by others. I myself am a dream. Dreams can't dream, can they?"

Kazumi laughs shyly to her friend. The red light of the façade blinks one last time and goes out, leaving the blue of the night to occupy the ceiling of the small apartment. The sound of the rain starts to come in through the window as if the light of the billboard had kept it out before. Iulana Romiszowska gets closer to Kazumi, envelops the feet of her friend, that disappear inside her big hands, and kisses each one of the small toes, before reaching for the first time for the nipples and mouth of the dancer.

Shining above everything, the full moon illuminates the vast white mattress of clouds that floats over Tokyo. For the moon, it's as if the city, the small apartment in Meguro, Kazumi, Iulana Romiszowska, her kisses and dreams, didn't exist.

14

URGENT
Attention: Mr. Atsuo Okuda
From: Suguro Shibata

I attach the partial transcript of phone communication #437, on 12.07.2013, that took place between the editors of *Literature Today* magazine, and your son, Mr. Shunsuke Okuda, between 19:12 and 19:40. The topic of the call is you, sir, Mr. Atsuo Okuda. We believe that after the publication of the interview last week, they will want to continue their pursuit of information about you, sir, using less elegant tactics, such as inconveniencing your son. I request guidance regarding what my actions should be from here forward. You will see, sir, that this will be necessary.

According to my records, Mr. Shunsuke, after leaving the foreigner at the subway station the afternoon of the trip to the zoo, when, according to the attached photos and video, he kissed her in public, he locked himself in his apartment, drank twelve cans of Asahi Dry beer and answered the following phone call, logged in our archives as #437 of the year 2013.

IT STARTS HERE:

" . . .?"

"Am I angry? How can I be angry at someone who never had anything to offer? It can't be personal."

" . . .?

"The old man is simply an empty fortress."

" . . .?"

"Mr. Okuda has already broken the neck of his femur, he has had eight ulcers, cancer of the eye, two heart attacks, and he is diabetic and has hypertension. And he doesn't die. He simply does not die.

He buried my mother and I don't doubt he'll bury all of us. Write that in your magazine."

" . . .?"

"Everything was always about him. The laurels for his poetry, the public recognition, the honor of the family name — nothing of this ever was transmitted to me or my mother. Many times we'd hear about it from the newspapers or the radio. He made a point of not sharing it with us."

" . . .?"

"The generous demeanor of a great public figure stayed outside the door. On the street he had the manners of a prince. At home, he was a despotic and violent egomaniac. What kind of poet can be a man like that?"

" . . .?"

"I don't know what I think of that. It gives me a headache just to think. Mr. Atsuo Okuda always called me Leech."

" . . .?"

"It starts with me, when I was eight, showing him an essay I had written in school and that the teacher had given the highest grade. The great name of Tanka poetry of Japan trashed my text inside and out. From the grammar to the images I used, on to the style. After a long verbal assault on the deficiencies of my prose, comparing it to Japanese literature of all times, from the Heian period to post-war, he said: 'Leech, you'll never amount to anything.' It was all about him."

" . . .?"

"I didn't cry in front of Mr. Okuda. I never cried while I took beatings for reasons like coming late to dinner or leaving something out of place in the living room. Not even when the great poet yanked me out of bed after having drunk half a bottle of uragasumi to recite a poem to me, or, more often, slap me around."

" . . .?"

"Yes, I remember the explosion of light in the room and the pres-

ence of a faceless specter that pulled me by the arms and dragged
me down the hall. My head would bounce against the door frame
while I was still half awake. In the beginning, I could tell if it was a
nightmare or not when my head hit the door frame. In my dreams, I
always saw my father as a large crustacean. With the deformed face
of a lobster and antennas that dragged on the floor. If I felt pain, it
was because in some way it was real, and his face slowly became
human after the beating. Today, sometimes, I see my father as a
human lobster."

"...?

"No, it made no difference."

"...?"

"I started to piss in my pants when Mr. Lobster Okuda arrived
after long trips to the interior. Once, the great crustacean poet noticed and said: "My son is a fairy. Look, woman, our son is a coward!
I should have picked another woman, because you were no good
even for that. Your blood is weak; the blame for the kid being like
this isn't mine. Or it could be that the worthless shit isn't my son. It
must be that, I wouldn't be surprised if this Leech wasn't mine ...""

"...?"

"When he hit me with a long piece of wood, Mr. Lobster Okuda
commanded me to cry."

"...?"

"Yes, cry like a fugu, he would say. Unlike him, who after the
beating sessions would lock himself in his room to cry alone, I never
took the bait. I developed a technique that served me my whole life,
of holding my tears in the bottom of my throat. The only time I cried
in front of Mr. Atsuo Okuda, the old man didn't notice. We were
in a Volvo sedan, returning from Shikoku Bay to Tokyo. The day
was clear; there were seagulls in the sky. My mother held a basket
of fish and her usual silence — she was an extinguished light who
only opened her mouth to eat increasingly smaller portions. Mr.
Lobster Okuda had caught an enormous fugu with the help of Mr.

Suguro Shibata, professor of the Association of the Harmonious Fugu of Tsukiji, who, by the way, must be listening to this tapped line. Good evening, Mr. Shibata . . . Well, my father loved to fish, cut, and eat *baiacus*, in spite of the danger, and Mr. Shibata taught him the technique. It was not just for the taste. He liked the fugu because it's the only fish that closes its eyes when it is cut open alive. And because the fugu makes a sound like the cry of a child when it is dying. My father studied for years, and he knows how to clean and filet a fugu and take out the poisonous parts of the fish. Even so, every time he forced us to eat it, I imagined he had left in some poison on purpose. Yes, that's how we lived. Write about it!"

". . .?"

"No, that afternoon I didn't think of the fugu's cry and I was timidly happy. I got in on the driver's side and climbed into the back seat of the two-door car. Without meaning to, or perhaps that's what I imagine, Mr. Lobster Okuda closed the door on my fingers. At that time cars had a very heavy frame. I spent the whole trip with my fingers crushed, trapped in the door. I didn't have the courage to say anything."

". . .?"

"Because of the obvious, the fault was mine. I had put my fingers there. Yes, the fault was mine. Now I ask, how can I, after such a thing, answer questions from the *Literature Today* magazine about the poetry of my father?"

". . .?"

"The curious thing is that Mr. Okuda already asked me that same question a few times. I was always a good reader. Since my early childhood, he introduced me to his lovers, and then, after describing his trysts to me in detail, he read me the beautiful poems that he wrote for each one of them. And he would ask: "What do you think, son?" only to throw my opinions into the garbage, like all the others. When I grew up, we even shared some of those sad women — Mr. Okuda would put them up to sleeping with me. He would sit on the edge of the bed with his fists under his chin, and while he watched us, he would write his poems right there, on long rolls of paper. This started when I was twelve and only stopped when I moved out. Afterwards, my father started to write poetry to my girlfriends, whom he knew about because he had people follow, record, photograph, and film us with hidden cameras.

"…?"

Yes, he still does it. Why wouldn't he?"

"…?"

"Yes, and there I believe I am telling you what you really want to know: Mr. Okuda never stopped writing. My father simply earned enough money not to have to deal with worms like you."

"…?"

"Yes, I'm very nervous. Yes, today I'm not being myself. Yes, it's terrible. Yes, you'll forgive me, but is there anything else I can add?"

"…?"

"The fifteen million yen doll?"

15

Last week Mr. Okuda spent a great deal of time in a hotel in the big city, taking care of secret business.

The few times he is home, he looks at the wall like a cat while I serve his tea. He has started to hear voices from I don't know where because they don't come from Mrs. Hiroko Okuda, the radio, the television, the Periscope Room, or from other human beings who sometimes knock on the door, like the man who opens his silver briefcase and delivers the envelopes with the disks and photos of Mr. Shunsuke, his son.

Mr. Okuda says his son is fifty years younger than he is, and he is an impertinent rascal who should respect him precisely because Mr. Okuda is fifty years older and has much less time ahead of him than his son has years on his back.

I didn't understand exactly what being younger or older means, since the other day Mr. Okuda said in a poem about my very white skin that past and future are the same thing said in different ways. That's why I committed the impertinence of directing my first question to Mr. Okuda, and I asked if "younger" and "older" are the same thing said in different ways.

Mr. Okuda was annoyed and said this could not be, because younger people have skin that is less wrinkled, and they are healthier, which means that they take longer to die. I asked why this happens, and Mr. Okuda explained it's because young people have less past, and that life ruins human beings as time goes on, and nothing can stop time.

I don't know exactly what time is.

Mr. Okuda tried to explain this to me and said that time is what separates the past from the future, and that to measure it there are instruments like watches and calendars, that are like little prisons, because nobody can escape from time, that it is the only thing that equalizes all human beings, along with death, of course, that walks in step with time — all the time.

And Mr. Okuda also told me that you say the word "now" when the past meets the future, in this moment, in the next, in the next, and so on, always at the frontier, fine as a strand of hair, between two stones that look very much alike: what still is and what will no longer be.

The name of this frontier is time, said Mr. Okuda.

Still not understanding very well what time was, I asked Mr. Okuda what death was, since it seems to me to be the same thing, only said in a different way. Mr. Okuda took a long sip of his tea, complained that it was colder than it should be, and then said that death is like being born backwards, or, returning to what one was before being born.

It's that, for me, death would be if he would lock me back into the box I came from and take away my name Yoshiko and leave me in there, alone in the dark, until I blended with the dark, and would not know what the dark is and what I am, and so I would lose the consciousness of my body and with it my body, which is what I am, because I am my body and my name Yoshiko, and that when you die you stop being what is and you become everything that is not, like a mountain that disappears, transforming into the landscape that surrounds it, losing the consciousness and the body of the mountain.

And he said, taking the last sip of tea, that the body of a human being rots and is eaten by insects if it is not burned like the body of Mrs. Hiroko Okuda, who I now keep inside me.

And also, that larvae will crack the porcelain of the irises of every human being in the western world, who do not have the custom of being cremated like we do, and that they will gnaw at the eyes of the living, until the world is slowly invaded by others who now are still dead and have not yet been born.

Mr. Okuda's words made a great impression on me.

While I retrieved the tray with the tea service from the small table, I felt as if the space between the ashes that exist inside me and the walls of my body emptied of air. For the first time, I had the strong desire to embrace my master, Mr. Okuda, as if in this way I could escape from time by hiding in Mr. Okuda the same way that Mrs. Okuda's ashes are hidden in my belly.

Later, in bed, I felt very alone. That's when I arrived at the conclusion, without understanding very well what time was, that it was something bad.

Last night I thought a lot about this, since unlike Mr. Okuda, I don't know how to sleep.

Thinking about time at night is like being lost in the labyrinth of Crete that I know through ancient stories that Mr. Okuda tells me. But here there is no string like Ariadne's to guide me to the exit. Those that appear on the path are false, and barely take me to a state of relief before I open the way to more desperate and dark regions of this labyrinth that exists in the middle of time until everything gets dark and the labyrinth and the dark that I keep inside me reveal themselves and capture me and the end comes.

Mr. Okuda stops snoring, turns his head toward the ceiling, and moves his eyes as if he is dreaming. Then, still asleep, he opens his eyes wide, looks at me and sees Mrs. Hiroko Okuda.

He embraces me, he touches me, I stick my first false string into the labyrinth, I try to forget time through Mr. Okuda.

16

The men from the office have given up calling me. From the sealed envelopes at the door of the house, I imagine that my absence has already caused me to be fired for just cause. I also imagine the comments in the hallways, the captains of that useless army of crabs saying: "I always thought he was a little strange," "he didn't socialize much with his colleagues," and "from now on maybe the spreadsheets will come out faster!" But this almost euphoric complicity will be ephemeral, rapidly substituted by fearful silences: "And what if I'm next?" And more: "When they fire me, what will they say about me?"

With the weight of these questions on their heads, they will finish their tea in a quick gulp and return like little fish in fishbowls to their desks, the little cages in the air in Kayabacho where they waste their lives as salarymen. Where I would be too, at a time like this, if I had not met a foreign woman that evening. What pity I feel for those poor guys who will never be with a woman like Iulana, with her great size. I don't care if I don't have a job. I am no longer a coward!

I am alone, after five cups of double shots of espresso, here in the cheap imitation of Dunkin' Donuts near the Shinjuku station, where I sat for the first time facing Iulana Romiszowska.

Since the gaijin refuses to give me her address or her phone number, this is the place where the minutes turn into entire afternoons of waiting. The attendants already know me, and every day we greet each other in silence. They know who I'm waiting for. When Iulana Romiszowska shows up, I feel the discreet looks of approval, as if they are relieved by her arrival.

The intervals between our encounters vary: sometimes she comes two days in a row, but afterwards a whole week can go by when she doesn't show up. On those empty days, like today, I sit with my little computer open, skimming the papers, flipping through web pages in a mechanical rhythm, concentrating on stories of death and crime, the only part of the news that really interests me, and now I am reading a recycled story that reminds me of Iulana: they found a dead woman on the banks of the Danube, a French woman twenty-two years old named Ophélie Bretnache. I think about who would be the Hamlet of this drowned Ofelia, whose Elsinore would be Budapest, in the same region of the world where my Polish-Romanian came from.

And this Ofelia in the news made me remember another one who was not Iulana, the Unknown Woman of the Seine, a French woman who had committed suicide, whose anonymous smile was immortalized in a plaster cast death mask commissioned by the pathologist of the morgue, who was so taken by the beauty of the young woman found in the river in 1901 — very near where, eighty years before, the famous cannibal Issei Sagawa honored his Japanese origins and devoured with passion another foreign woman, this one Dutch, a classmate of his in the literature program at the Sorbonne.

Death, as Mr. Lobster Okuda often says, is photogenic. In addition to inspiring Rilke and Nabokov and being photographed by Man Ray, the face of the Unknown Woman of the Seine started to adorn buildings — it hung for decades on the wall of my father's study, and today it is on the door of the Periscope Room. Besides this, it has been transformed into a mold for the face of the dolls in first aid training schools around the world — according to Mr. Okuda, with so much mouth-to-mouth, she has become the most kissed woman of all time. If I told this story to Iulana Romiszowska, who has already been kissed a lot, certainly more than I have kissed other women, I imagine she'd say something like:

"It makes sense, Shun! I inevitably turn men into Hamlets . . ."

Or at least that's what the copy of the foreign woman I carry in my head says, making comments all the time on what I think and see.

In the café, before I begin to imagine how to interrupt Iulana's walk in the direction of her future lovers, the strangers she will kiss when I become just a small chapter among her many memories, and still, as if I could do this imitating Sagawa and his foreigner in Paris, a door opens forcefully, and right away I see myself with no connection whatsoever to the news in front of me, with Shakespeare, Mr. Okuda, or with the living human beings of this or any other place, because the person entering the café now is Iulana Romiszowska.

She orders a croissant and a double espresso. She swallows everything with no manners, like a famished animal. Then she asks about my family.

"Do you have siblings? What are their names? Who were your parents?"

"Why do you want to know all of this?"

"Sometimes I think I know very little about you."

In the measure that I refuse to discuss my private life, she starts to tell me about her childhood, how her mother was indifferent to her and her father, the melomanic Polish consul, who would take her to concerts, and how that was the great window of communication between them. She starts to talk about the fascination of her father for romantics like Shostakovich, and she begins to cite some of his piano pieces, Brahms sonatas and Schumann's "Carnival," which remind her of the old man saying they were antidotes for the technology oriented and mechanical world in which they lived, for the *scientific* era that the century had brought, and how ironic she had ended up in Tokyo, what would the old man think of this place? I smile silently remembering Misako, daughter of an ignorant industrialist, incapable of this or any other kind of conversation.

"What's so funny, Shun?"

I say it's nothing, and she keeps talking about Mr. Romiszowska, how he was tall, strong, and intelligent, how she disappeared into the old man's lap. His father had died heroically defending Vilnius, today the capital of Lithuania, when Poland was invaded by the Soviets in 1939, and at this moment I can hardly disguise my envy of those dead men.

As soon as I was alone, I hurried to buy tickets to a piano recital in Kan-I Hoken Hall, in Gotanda — I counted on the luck that she would show up the next day.

I had been just a few times to a concert like this, but often enough to know that before you buy tickets it's necessary to make an important choice: what side of the hall to sit in. If we sit far enough to the left, we get a good view of the white and black keys of the instrument, and the movement of the hands and the hammering of the fingers of the pianist on them.

On the other hand, if we buy seats to the right of the piano, we will not see the keys or the hands of the soloist, but his expressions: the arched eyebrows accompanying the dynamics of the music, the shoulders and neck in a pendulum movement that will follow the ostinatos, the moving score formed by lines of the forehead contracted into short spasms, the blinking of the eyes marking time like a metronome, the movement of the feet over the pedals — everything that makes us imagine that it is that human being who is responsible for the sound we hear, even though we can't really see him playing.

Sometimes we can see, in the elevated top of the piano, and only if it's well polished, the undular and inverted reflection of the backs of the pianist's hands dancing over the keyboard like the shadow of two crows that the yellow light of a lamppost imprints on a dark night. Or like the foreign woman, who behind a veil of silence and incomprehension, smiles at me.

Iulana Romiszowska, unlike the rest, always makes me sit on the right side of the theater.

17

What we see now is the first meal we share in a Korean restaurant in Odaiba. Behind the outline of Iulana Romiszowska's blond, messy hair, the bay shines in tones of blue, sparkling in millions of minuscule mirrors in movement in the thread of water. From here, the perpetual flow of cars and trains over the bridge of Tokyo is soft, the city looks like an inoffensive toy.

I take a piece of raw meat to the Korean grill with the *hashi*, and while I wait, I drink an Asahi beer and watch the smoke rise in a straight line to the metal exhaust fan. This image distracts me and I almost don't notice, behind the fatty cloud that takes over the space between me and Iulana Romiszowska, that the specter of Mr. Lobster Okuda approaches the table.

My father, his hair and beard completely white, wears a kimono with the family insignia on it, wooden sandals, and on his nose he wears a pair of round dirty glasses. In his right hand he carries a lobster mask with antenna and rubber claws dragging on the ground.

A foreigner this time, son?

Mr. Lobster Okuda always picked the least appropriate times to invade my reality, but to disrespect the first meal that I share with Iulana Romiszowska in a Korean restaurant in Odaiba is something completely off limits.

Oh, what the ashes of your dead mother whisper into my ears!

To disguise my irritation in seeing the ghost of my living father, a faded and badly finished reflection of myself, I ask the waiter for another beer. Every time I see old people, especially my father, I feel that I am no more or less closer to death than any one of them, and this leaves me profoundly unsettled: they make me think that perhaps I have aged before my body.

Mr. Lobster Okuda, as always, ignores me and declaims, without meter, terrible verses behind Iulana's shoulders:

Shunsuke, behold!
Behind the irises
of Iulana Romiszowska
Her orbits hold
Air squadrons
Tigers lurking in ambush
Water clocks
The light fades in those Russian eyes
And the time of those clocks is dishonest
And the time of those clocks is obscene

Iulana Romiszowska, like the other customers in the restaurant, is incapable of seeing the apparition of Mr. Okuda. Without dropping her eyes from her gaze outside the room, she removes her chin from the palm of her left hand and drinks an apple soda. She dilates her nostrils while she sucks the liquid rising through a straw. She closes her mouth in a small circle, stretching the white skin of her cheeks.

Learn to see
The geometric construction
Of the workers, Shun!
The workers who sculpted the features
And carved the curve of the lips
of Iulana Romiszowska
The workers who opened with hoes
Her marble veins
The workers who on her skin forgot:
A shovel, a hammer
A wooden stump, a stair
A saw!

For a brief moment, I imagine myself recognizing *the territory of the beams of that body with trembling fingers, like a blind man who reads the gospels in Braille,* and I stick my fingers in the direction of her hair, *scaled like liana vines by the small suicidal workers,* but I quickly chase away these idiotic ideas, nonsense whispered in my ear by Mr. Lobster Okuda.

"Bullshit, Dad!"

I toss another glass of cold beer and concentrate on erasing Mr. Lobster Okuda from my head and thinking about other things, exchanging his image for eels, metal structures, lab monkeys, or astrolabes. The workers who *sculpted the features and carved the curve of Iulana's lips* are unaware of my efforts, and they try to attach themselves to the freckles of the foreign woman before throwing themselves on the sizzling grill with smiles on their faces.

When I think Mr. Lobster Okuda has finally disappeared, I hear a shout. A shout that is not from any microscopic worker hanging on Iulana Romiszowska. A shout that is also not from one of the waiters or the other customers. It's my father, who reappears behind Iulana Romiszowska and starts to dance Awa-Odori steps around the table.

Now he is wearing the lobster mask with the long antenna that drag on the floor, he circles the table and sings, jumping and pointing at my companion:

Ah,
You're a criminal!
You're bad!
And I . . .
I'm a monster
A shameful aberration
You would have a fever if you could
Look at yourself the way I see you

The way I see the workers and their hard hats with lights
Walking through gardens of cherry trees in bloom

The workers who touched the inside of your veins
Who sank to their knees in your concrete
Who sculpted your ivory bones
The workers who raised the great void
And the great absence that is you
(How many doors that lead to rooms
Where Shunsuke will never enter!)
The workers who chewed and furrowed
The wood of your shadows
Who climbed into your half open mouth
Hanging on cables
In the illuminated gallery that opens up
Wherever you go

The workers of your sad childhood
Crying hidden under the living room table
In the port city of the Black Sea
Constanța, land of long corridors
of emptiness and uninhabited corners

The workers who opened up landscapes and rocky islands
on the leaden seas of your body
The wrinkly elbow, the pale armpits
The sacred spaces between your toes

The workers who know the horizon
That you keep as a secret

I envy the quick and glorious
Existence of the workers
Who built symmetry into the disorder
of Iulana Romiszowska

The workers are as jealous as I am
One day, when she's asleep,
They will escape from your body and kill me
Like someone who treads on a rotten branch

If I'm lucky!

Mr. Okuda-crustacean-poet makes a rapid bow and flies out the picture window in the direction of the bay that shines in tones of blue, sparkling in millions of minuscule mirrors in movement in the thread of water. After flying over the small replica of the Statue of Liberty of Odaiba, his ghost joins the almost imperceptible movement of the cars and trains over the Tokyo Bridge until it disappears into the city. The echo of his words dies quickly in the landscape.

I turn my eyes back to Iulana Romiszowska, relieved that she had not noticed what had just happened here. I stretch my arm across the table, and the foreign woman interrupts me with her open hand in the air.

"Don't start. Don't look at me that way . . ."

"What way?"

"Like that. With all that *tenderness*."

"What's the problem?"

"The problem is I don't like it, that's all."

The smoke rises from the grill. I feed the machine with more pieces of raw meat. We eat in silence. Suddenly Iulana extends her hand over the grill, as if she were going to place her palm on the red hot surface. The sun seems to shine more brightly outside the window that separates us from the rest of the world. A motorcycle goes down the street making noise.

"I hate my hand."

"Your hand is pretty."

"I want to have slender fingers like Japanese women."

"Nonsense. I had a girlfriend from Kyoto who had fingers thicker than a rhinoceros's."

"Or then the fingers of a pianist."

"Only pianists need fingers of pianists. And you don't know how to play the piano."

"Would you like it if I could play the piano like that concert pianist? I know you thought she was pretty."

"It doesn't really make any difference to me."

"Of course that's not true! Imagine coming home and listening to a Rachmaninoff piece played by your wife in a nightgown!"

"I never thought of it that way."

"Well you should, Shun. You should find that woman, that delicate Japanese pianist. Because with these thick ugly fingers, I never . . ."

Iulana Romiszowska's forehead turns into a complicated pattern of furrows. I hold her left hand, still floating dangerously a few centimeters from the hot grill, and I envelop it in mine as if it were a dead bird. I try to forget the workers spread all over Iulana's skin, and I kiss the tip of each of her fingers, and the space between them, without minding the other customers of the restaurant who are now concentrating their attention on the table of the strange couple. One of us says:

"Let's go."

While we wait for the subway, under the eye of the submarine camera of Mr. Okuda in a suspended giraffe-station of reinforced concrete full of tourists from the interior, Iulana wraps herself around my torso like a squid attacking its prey. The mountain of flesh and rosy skin then kneels and, almost with her knees on the ground, she leans her head on my chest:

"Is your heart mine, baby Shun?"

18

Separated from me, from Iulana Romiszowska, and from the reinforced concrete subway giraffe-station by eight hours and twenty-two minutes on the time line, twelve other stations that leave from Odaiba and 4,543 meters of underway passages, is the Shinjuku Hyatt Regency, a brown marble box with square windows.

We see the line of taxis stopped at the hotel entrance and, behind the revolving door, a mastodon crystal chandelier floating above the great atrium. We see, in front of the concierge desk, smiling workers dressed in black, ready to greet any visitor in five different languages. We also see, giving access to the suites, four clear tubes where the panoramic elevators go up and down and that take us to the carpeted corridors of the twelfth floor, where behind the locked door of room 1212 with the "Do Not Disturb" sign, there is a circle of light on a square table.

This circle has its origins in a smaller one, placed less than a meter above. From a lateral angle, we see that the circle above the table is the base of a cone of light that starts on its surface and ends in a metal lamp hanging from the ceiling. The smoke produced by a hand-rolled cigarette runs through the opaque air of the cone. Holding the cigarette before putting it out in the ashtray we can't see, is the right hand of Mr. Lobster Okuda.

We don't see the ashtray because the ashtray is outside of the circle of light on the square table. We don't see anything that is not part of the cone of light, and this includes the view to the towers of the city hall with the look of a cubist cathedral, of the three pyramids of the Park Hyatt and of the park and skyline of Shinjuku that we would see if the curtains were open. And we also can't see a black telephone, the arms, legs, trunk, and kimono and practically the whole body of my father, with the exception of his right hand, that now lifts the cigarette to the ashtray we can't see. No light enters through the window or under the door.

The table, the cone of light, the cigarette, the kimono, and the body of Mr. Okuda are in a room above the other eleven, piled one on top of the other, and under thirteen more, equally positioned on the same vertical principle. Mr. Okuda does not like to have thirteen floors over his head, and he thinks every day about moving to another room, higher than this one where there is a circle of light on a square table.

But at this moment there are other priorities. Mr. Lobster Okuda has decided to implement his plan, which is to wake up the dancer Kazumi, who shares an apartment in Meguro with Iulana Romiszowska.

When the phone rings, Kazumi will not remember that she was dreaming of occupying Iulana Romiszowska's body.

In the dream, the first she will have remembered in years, Kazumi looks at herself (she looks at Iulana's body) in the mirror above the sink of public restroom 14B at the north entrance of the Shinjuku station, at zero minutes on the timeline and 1,690 meters from the lobby of the Hyatt Regency, where eleven floors up, there is a circle of light on a square table.

Kazumi lifts her blouse, and two breasts much bigger and heavier than hers appear imprinted against the cold surface of the mirror. The dancer feels the weight of these large breasts on her back and a light burning in the pink nipples. Before she decides if what she feels is really pain, she notices Iulana's look, through which Kazumi can see *herself*, imprisoned in the body of her friend.

It's the dead look of a doll. *Her* cloudy eyes are like marbles.

At the moment when Kazumi becomes frightened by the eyes that imprison her behind their sockets, Mr. Lobster Okuda finishes dialing her number on the black telephone we can't see.

The phone rings pulling Kazumi at the same time (1) from the dream, (2) from Iulana Romiszowska's body, and (3) from the bathroom at the north entrance of the Shinjuku station. After the call wakes her up, the bathroom mirror will start to reflect the tiles on the immobile wall until someone goes back in.

"Who is it?" Kazumi looks at the digital clock that blinks 04:43 am in red.

"You know who it is."

"What do you want?"

"Are you on something to speak to me in that tone of voice? Are you crazy?"

"I'm sorry sir, it's late."

"I ring you up wanting to give you good news . . . your cats send you a hug."

"Did you do anything to them? Are they all right?"

"I want news about Shunsuke and the foreign woman."

"I should know something by tomorrow. The gaijin isn't saying anything."

" . . . "

"OK?"

"You're not forgetting anything?"

"When?"

"Tomorrow. You can come after six in the evening."

" . . . "

"Don't forget the ropes."

On the mattress a little above the mat where Kazumi talks on the phone, Iulana Romiszowska has the pillow over her head. She could only understand the word "gaijin" from the conversation. The lights that blink on the façade of the building fill the room with a reddish cloud. Outside, the wet asphalt reflects the towers and shop windows in tones of silver.

19

I didn't take long to discover that Iulana Romiszowska has a child's nipples but a pussy as big and wide as a cavern, because it had been much used by dozens of gaijin who had been there before me. A Japanese woman, even if she is the oldest whore of Yoshiwara, is a tight glove. But the European woman, as I learned after I met Iulana, is hollow. She has no bottom.

Having that big, hollow woman gave me an unfamiliar sensation of power. After Iulana Romiszowska, sex with Japanese women seemed incestuous.

She has no shyness at all. Mr. Okuda Crustacean would say that when she takes off her clothes it's as if she hadn't been wearing anything at all. Her body is a collection of abstract shapes that places itself over me and defoliates quickly.

I feel the weight in my shoulders pressed into the mat of my room where, with us, are all the westerners who have already used Iulana. They take turns, embodied within me. When we're done, this animal that is the foreign woman gets up dripping between her legs. She expels what she carries inside her over my mouth and throat.

"Open your mouth, Shun!"

And she discharges the come from all those men onto my face until the whole room is soaked in a sticky broth. Afterwards she walks to the window. I quickly close the curtains.

"Why? I never close the curtains at my house . . . What's the problem if they see me naked?"

And she turns her face to me with a perverse look, the dappled light of the afternoon on her ivory breasts. Mr. Lobster Okuda whispers behind the reflection of the glass:

You know . . .
There'll be no way out
Except to kill her.

20

The couple gains intimacy. We start to treat each other, on even days, as if we were our parents: I was her father, the melomaniac diplomat; she was my mother, timid and dead.

This game takes up entire afternoons of surrender and also long cold spells, when any approach of mine is received with profound disgust — she has already vomited on the record player and on the toilet seat. At those times she says she doesn't need me for anything, that I am useless and insufficient for her infinite desires, and insinuates stories of her past in foreign lands, telling me about all the westerners of different sizes and colors that had rubbed against her lips and that she had made gush into all the orifices of her body.

Minutes later she begs forgiveness in her well-pronounced university English, she says she's inventing stories to get my attention, and, in an attack of jealousy for ex-girlfriends of mine whom she has created, she bites my mouth or throws a blender out the window.

It also happens that we address each other with switched names: she calls me Iulana and I call her Shunsuke. In this game we tell terrible secrets to each other, secrets we promise to forget the next day. I will never be able to free myself of them, as they have been recorded by the machines of the submarine installed here in the house.

Iulana Romiszowska will not have the same problem. She will not remember a single sentence, because she doesn't give much importance to what people say, always receiving my reply in an obtuse way, interrupting what I say with her open hand over my mouth.

Already the first night together in my apartment, without having decided to do it, we slept with arms, legs, and tentacles intertwined. Two squid tangled in strange combinations, coordinated by specific rules but not rehearsed, such as, for example, changing the positions of our bodies in the middle of the night.

(When my fingers go to sleep and I feel the need to turn to the other side in bed, a subtle movement to disengage my arm from Iulana Romiszowska's neck would unleash a series of complex movements, and we, in a few seconds, would resume our embrace in the opposite position: (1) Iulana's arm on my chest, (2) my left leg under her right thigh, (3) her left knee tucked into my left leg, (4) holding hands in geometric patterns, (5) the nose of the Russian warming a specific part of my neck.)

On one of those black nights, full of wonder and panic, I will have an interminable dream while Iulana Romiszowska embraces me from behind.

In it, I am also lying down, but on the stairwell of the Reiyukai Shakaden, holding the decapitated head of Mr. Lobster Okuda. The black mouth of the temple closes its teeth on me. I run until I fall at the Roppongi intersection, where the neon arteries transform into whips that lash me. The blacks, the Chinese whores, and drunken foreigners tear with their claws at the concrete cartilage of the buildings and throw the pieces at me. The ground turns into an escalator going the wrong direction. I see a plush cat with empty eyes destroy the viaduct with an enormous metal bone. When the larvae start coming out of the cat's eyes, it asks me questions in Romanian, and I wake up with Iulana Romiszowska's fingers around an erection.

It doesn't take me long to realize it's my piece of flesh that she wraps in her cold hand.

Iulana nests her thighs on my legs and, sitting on my knees, facing me, she stares at a fixed point between my eyes. In the middle of the white pillows of her breasts that escape from the half open shirt, occasionally revealing a straying pink nipple, there is a crucifix. I think of how absurd it is to wear a semi-naked dying man around your neck, but I don't say anything.

She stretches her arm over my throat and gropes for the gun in her bag. She points it to my forehead and then between my balls:

"Who does this hard cock belong to, my baby Shun?"

And she pulls off her panties tossing them aside. In one of the rare moments that Iulana lets me dominate her, I mount her from above. She remains with her knees together and folded, pressed against her inert head. She appears to feel nothing, in spite of my efforts. Sooner or later, something happens, because the foreign woman starts to tremble and a fillet of blood starts to run down the corner of her mouth.

Maybe I am still dreaming.

Because now I am walking down a dark hallway, and then in another, and there is no more blood on the sheets. Iulana Romiszowska is now a door. A green door with a sculptured clam over it, a small window with an iron grate, seven vertical wooden arrows, and in the middle, a rusted lock.

I crouch down, rest my outspread hands on my knees and look through the keyhole of the door that is Iulana. I see a rectangular hangar with white walls and cathedral ceilings that recede out of sight. In front of the walls are dozens of workers occupied with making notes and cataloging the works of a museum that only exhibits white paintings. They face the walls like children being sent to the corner.

When I wake up, definitely or not, she is standing with her hands on her waist, her feet turned out, her head inclined to the left, her forehead covered with blond bangs, dressed in my shirt with all the buttons open except the last one that covers the carelessly shaved sex of Iulana Romiszowska.

"You've slept too long, Shun!"

After going to the bathroom, I turn on the sound system and put on a recording.

"Do you remember we heard this when we had coffee the first time?"

"I think so. This music goes with the morning."

"It's not true. It goes with the dawn."

The submarine captures a few seconds of silence between us. Iulana Romiszowska, as always, stares at a fixed point between my eyes.

"You don't hear it? The voice of the Brazilian musician João Gilberto is a nocturnal voice."

"How's that?"

"When it's very late, the city is turned off and people are at home, you notice they naturally speak in a low tone?"

"Yes."

"It's a voice that you only use with someone you're intimate with."

"Shun?"

"What?"

"Maybe one day we can talk to each other with our nocturnal voices."

I make coffee and toast and fry two eggs for her. I don't eat any of that; my breakfast is rice with raw egg. Iulana makes a face of disgust and runs her large fingers through my hair with a look of pity. The smell of the coffee and the rice, combined with the stuffy air and the smell of mildew, gives the room an opaque texture. Sitting at opposite corners of the small table, we look at each other in silence while the Brazilian musician João Gilberto sings in his nocturnal voice.

What we see now, through the periscope, is our first breakfast.

In that moment I would not know to put it that way, but sleeping with Iulana Romiszowska was enough for me to know that I would never again be accustomed to the solitude, without company or not, of before. With this realization, would come the suspicion that the rest of the world must have disappeared, my father and the submarine, while we were in there — a suspicion that could be graphically represented by the dark halo surrounding the house.

I walk to the balcony and open the curtain, lighting up the room.

Through the window I see the gray smudge of the Daikanyama neighborhood, where I live in an apartment purchased by Mr. Lobster Okuda in the 1960s, before the place became pricey, now an agglomeration of galleries and cafés where the trendsetters talk about everything in the world that doesn't interest me.

Everything is *still* there.

Iulana Romiszowska clears the table, turns on the hot water, and starts to wash the dishes. Now she is not a door, a sphinx, an inexpressive reflection in the mirror with doll's eyes, or a hangar with white walls, but an almost unknown and semi-naked woman to whom I could offer, immediately, my life and my death.

While the stranger washes the dishes, I sniff my fingers and smell the bittersweet musk of Iulana Romiszowska's body. I lock all the doors of the house, throw the keys out the window, and close the curtains — I want to change the world into a black halo to escape it and take Iulana Romiszowska with me. This is the only escape possible: never to leave.

21

The night of that same morning, we will walk through the streets of Roppongi after going to the movies. Since Iulana Romiszowska is taller than I am, holding hands is inconvenient when we walk: my hand will always be under Iulana's thick fingers, which forces me to raise my forearm subtly to reach the woman's hand. After a few minutes this arrangement becomes uncomfortable and I prefer to wrap my arm around my companion's waist, always taking care to be on the higher side of the sidewalk.

Iulana Romiszowska, who is unaware of these strategies, notices an exotic neon sign on the sixth floor of a building.

"What's that, Shun?"

"It's an Egyptian café."

"I want to go to the Egyptian café. Will you invite me?"

I look at my watch and see that it's already tomorrow. I nod yes – I'll probably never work again on any day that follows. The elevator door opens to a dark anteroom where a fat doorman in a bowler hat greets us as he opens a padded door. The café consists of one single space, with low sofas and pillows on the floor. On the walls, there are mirrors framed with neon wires under arabesques painted on the ceiling. In a corner a jukebox plays J-pop on high volume.

All around, drunken people tell stories they've never told before.

Under the cloud of smoke generated by the shishas, we ask for green tea and strawberry tobacco. Iulana sucks the air through the tube and releases smoke through her dilated nostrils with the ease of a professional. I take pride in the appearance of this woman (1) as if her body, hairdo, features, and clothing not only belonged to me, but were a part of me; (2) as if all the stares at Iulana Romiszowska were directed at me; (3) as if the small panties of the Polish woman had infiltrated hidden corners of my flesh; and finally, (4) as if her memories belonged to me by right.

The thought that there will always be new memories of this woman to be restituted to me causes a slight tremor when Iulana passes the shisha pipe to me. She is a well of experiences outside of this island, and with countless strangers. Perhaps one of them is the westerner wearing a worn leather jacket who approaches the sofa where we are sitting and says Iulana Romiszowska's name, with the perfect pronunciation I will never be capable of producing.

"Yes?" — she avoids looking up.

"Do you remember me?"

"Who are you?"

"You don't remember me?"

"I don't know you."

The man in the leather jacket looks at Iulana Romiszowska in silence, while he finishes the glass of whiskey that he holds in his left hand. After thirty-five seconds clocked by the submarine, he leaves his empty glass on the table before turning around and disappearing.

"Who is that man?"

"I don't know."

"You know."

"I don't know, Shun!"

"You know who he is. I know that you know, and you know you are lying to me. Why do you lie to me?"

"You're crazy."

"You're a slut."

Bang! Iulana Romiszowska makes my head swivel with a slap, throws the shisha on the ground and the hot tea on my clothes. Minutes later, the pedestrians on the sidewalk, where a few minutes ago Iulana Romiszowska had asked, "What is that, Shun?" pointing to an exotic neon sign on the sixth floor, would force themselves to pretend that they do not see a man in a wet suit clinging to the knees of a gaijin, dragging himself along the sidewalk to beg her forgiveness and to say that he loves her.

22

I haven't washed my hands in four days.

Today I got into the shower with plastic gloves and rubber bands on my wrists. And I also used gloves to eat, handle money, phones, and the subway pass, push elevator buttons, type on the computers at home and in the cafés.

I protect my hands because between the flesh of my fingers and my nails there is a silent battle going on between the particles of Iulana Romiszowska and the particles of the planet earth. The particles of the planet earth try to expel the particles of Iulana. The smell of her panties and of her cavities lasts exactly four and a half days on my fingers.

Then it disappears. And I need to find her again.

"What is that on your hands?"

Here she is, in the same cheap imitation of Dunkin' Donuts near the Shinjuku station where we came when she was still the woman who would succeed Misako and where we heard together, for the first time, the Brazilian musician João Gilberto sing with his nocturnal voice. Today Iulana wants me to take her to Akihabara because she wants to buy a camera.

"Why do you want a camera?"

"Why do you think? To dig a hole? Of course it's to take pictures, Shun."

"Of what?"

"I want to take pictures of that bridge in Marunouchi, where we walked yesterday."

"The Tokiwa-bashi Bridge. What's there?"

"I like to see the color of the reflection of the water on the viaduct."

"You're going to buy a camera just because you like a color?"

"Are you going to help me or not?"

We take the subway. Under the slanted stares of the crowd (they imagine that Iulana is one of those Russian models who end up as whores in Japan, and I am a salaryman with exotic taste), we make the pilgrimage to Akihabara. Iulana prefers to stand. I lean the weight of my body on the umbrella. In front of us, an adolescent concentrates intently on texting on a cell phone. Across from us, an elderly couple plays double Sudoku. The LCD monitors advertise products, the next stations, the weather conditions. The rain should stop before we arrive.

The train stops.

The landscape that we see through the window stops being a blur of horizontal lines to freeze into illuminated shapes backlit the rain. Next to the bridge where the Yamanote line passes, there is a wall of buildings and commercial galleries. On top of everything, a big billboard advertises soup in neon lights. The only set of windows without closed curtains or darkened glass is on the fifth floor of the curved building to the right. There, a group of little ballerinas rehearse a dance in the middle of the room, while others stretch their legs on a metal barre. The movement of the girls is so *pure* that I think of tapping Iulana Romiszowska on the shoulder and sharing the ballerinas with her.

The movement of my hand to her body is interrupted when, after a jerk, the composition starts to move again. In an instant, the ballerinas cease to exist.

Iulana Romiszowska ascends the escalator of BIC Camera on the stair in front of me. She wears the short shorts in fashion with the Japanese women and that on her are completely obscene. Since Iulana is not capable of understanding a tenth of what is going on around her, she doesn't notice the looks that follow her, the crude comments of the old men, and the jokes of the school kids.

I want all of these conspirators to die in an explosion on the subway.

The fifth floor of the department store is the usual pandemonium of electronic signals, jingles, and endless aisles, one for each type of product. Everything is labeled: the brand, the model, and the price. There is not an hour of the day or night when the place is not filled with people, also wearing labels more or less visible on their clothing, shoes, and bags.

While I distract myself with a camera with a motion detector attached to the shutter release button, Iulana unhitches her waist from my left hand and does a disappearing act that I only notice minutes later, when a child in a cap tugs at the cuff of my pants and extends an electronic toy to me.

She wants to show me something blinking on the small screen and I want her to return to the uterus that she came from. Where is Iulana? Like someone dozing at dawn on the sofa with the TV on, I wake up with a disagreeable jolt and start to look for her by scanning the illuminated showcases of the department store. An idea gives me immediate relief: it won't be hard to find Iulana Romiszowska, even in the middle of this crowd, because she is at least ten centimeters taller than any of us.

That's not what happens. After fifteen minutes, I consider the notion of having someone announce Iulana Romiszowska's name on the store loudspeaker. It would be a disaster: the sales clerk would not be able to pronounce the name even if I wrote it phonetically on a piece of paper. And Iulana would not understand the message. We are stranded from each other, and I start to consider other possibilities: Iulana simply could have decided to stop being with me.

If that's true, it will be impossible to find her in this interminable city. I don't have her address and Iulana Romiszowska has stopped working at the Abracadabrar, the club where I met her on the fourth floor of a building from the 1970s, on one of the main streets of Kabukicho — since we started seeing each other regularly, I started paying her double the salary she earned so she wouldn't work anymore and would spend nights with me.

Before putting the submarine into action, which would force me to resume contact with Mr. Lobster Okuda, I could do a search through similar clubs, that number in the thousands in an area of a few blocks — in some cases, there are dozens on the same floor of rundown buildings or at the back of galleries in dark areas of the neighborhood. Besides this, she could start working not as a waitress in an escort bar, but at Wendy's, at Starbucks, or an Irish pub, or who knows where.

Or, this too: she could start renting her body, which she swore to me she had not done since she arrived in Japan. She could do this with immediate success in one of the Ginza nightclubs that offer western women from Eastern Europe.

There were still intermediate options: (1) serve drinks pantiless in a bar with mirrors on the floor, (2) dress up as a teacher and offer her breasts to men dressed up as babies, (3) cover herself with a leather corset with an opening at the crotch and defecate on her clients (she could only eat rice and fish if she decided to do this), (4) go to a swing club and rent herself to couples, (5) sell her time inside a store window and talk half-naked with men through the intercom while she studies Japanese, and (6) specialize in role switching and insert rubber phalluses and her own tongue into young men squatting on an anatomically designed chair made for this purpose.

Or, finally, she could go back to her native city or to the countries of Europe where she has lived and take up with her old lovers in Constanța, a port city on the Black Sea, or in Bucharest, where she studied art history, or in Paris and Berlin, where she lived before coming to Tokyo, and in every one of these cities reencounter the men who still keep in their memories the touch of her fingers and of her tongue.

23

When I'm on one of the corners of Akihabara, Mr. Lobster Okuda shows up asking for Iulana under the spaghetti of neon where fat girls with lace-trimmed skirts, white aprons, bobby socks, and little caps distribute ads for *maid cafés* to the juvenile perverts who buy and sell electronic scrap on the sidewalks.

Mr. Okuda-Crustacean, ignored by the crowd, reminds me of one of those guys who wear plush suits in theme parks. He climbs onto an exhaust duct and begins his chant:

Ask yourself, Shunsuke, my leech
What they would say in Romanian
The first neolatin language
Created on the banks of the Danube
After the Romans there forgot
Latin that had mixed with Dacian
The slave lexicon and Balkan verbs?

After father grunts out these senseless phrases, I notice that on the other side of the street, lined up with the crowd that waits for the light to change, is the enormous Cyclops eye of the Gyodai monster, the enlarger of the monsters of the interplanetary empire Daiseidan Gozuma.

What would they say in Romanian
That sharp, dry language
What would she say (said, will say)
With her hands busy
Her knees planted on the ground
Looking overhead?

Around the enormous eye there are what seem to be the lips of an open mouth that occupies the entire diamond-shaped face of the monster Gyodai. And not just the lips, but the pointed teeth and the overlapping layers of exposed cartilage. His body is covered by brown scales, and he is the height of an average Japanese human being, and the width of three average Japanese human beings. The two feet of the monster that enlarges monsters of the interplanetary empire Daiseidan Gozuma are thick, and they leave a trail of slime on the sidewalk. His arms are two long grasshopper claws that the monster uses for balance, as if they were canes. Suddenly the monster Gyodai points them in the direction of Mr. Okuda while he unleashes a multicolored ray from his big eye and says:

"Gyodai, yai, yai, yai."

The light changes, freeing the pedestrian fury of the crowd, and the monster Gyodai is left alone on the median. Anticipating the nefarious consequences of that eye pointed at my father, I run in Gyodai's direction, and in the middle of the street, I see it's too late. The beam of blue light projected on Mr. Lobster Okuda has an immediate effect: the old man rolls his eyes and trembles as if suffering an epileptic attack. Then, he starts to grow from the feet up, in an expanding process that also affects his legs, trunk, arms, lobster head, and antennas dragging on the ground.

In a few seconds, father has grown bigger than the lights on top of the buildings of Akihabara.

The passersby only notice what is happening when Mr. Lobster Okuda's weight produces cracks in the asphalt that rapidly spread through the city blocks. The scene is opened by a woman's scream. Some hurry away but most don't move. They look up while they photograph and film my father with their cellular phones and digital cameras.

They seem relieved: finally, for the first time in their lives, *something* is happening. Something *real*. This sensation must be worth the risk of having your body crushed by the feet, antenna, and imprudent gestures of Mr. Okuda.

Contrary to the young crowd, the old people, survivors of a

pre-occidental, purified world, in which things still exist such as shadows, the hands of clocks, bombs, and hunger, start running unashamedly through the streets, carrying ruins inside themselves.

A group of adolescents next to me says things like:

"Wow! Is this a trailer for a film? Look how cool! He is *really* awesome!"

Even if the buildings fall around them, and the broken windows of the Styrofoam constructions eject human beings, and the lights of the avenue crash onto the pavement creating a carpet of small glass shards and blood, the *otaku* will continue at the Akihabara intersection taking pictures of the disaster with outstretched arms. They will register the images of their own deaths.

In two days, the police will find the pictures, when they are able to separate from the bloody mass of flesh intact memory cards inside crushed cameras, as if they were organs of cyborgs that had invaded the crowd.

The Gyodai monster looks with satisfaction at his seventy-meter-high creation, and before it is surrounded by a group of *otaku* youth asking for autographs and pictures, he runs away from there with small little steps, supported on his cane-arms. Mr. Lobster Okuda Giant Crustacean resumes the declamation of his poetry, now with a deafening voice that shatters the few windows and shop fronts that are still left in one piece:

What would be the words
She would say in her nocturnal voice
The large bones against the sweat
Of men invading her entrails?

What would be, precisely,
The secret words
Of Iulana Romiszowska?

It's time to calm down Mr. Okuda. I impound a megaphone and tell him that, without taking into account the hypothesis that Iulana Romiszowska has left Tokyo and escaped the surveillance of the submarine, the next man can, at this moment, be in any part of the city. We might, as a matter of fact, run into him in the street, sit in the same café, share the same subway car. We are in the same earthly atmosphere, the sun that shines on my face is also his sun, the lights and the cartilage of concrete that surround us are the same.

He, the next one, would run into Iulana at the exit of the movies and say something polite, and after a few furtive encounters, he would exploit the flesh of our woman in a love motel on a hill in Shibuya. And she would go home with wet hair, holding in her arms a bouquet of white lilies as if she were holding a baby.

Yes, Mr. Okuda, certainly there must exist someone whose body fits into the lacunae of Iulana Romiszowska better than ours, whose temperament is more suited to her silences and whims, another to rest his arm on her shoulder in interminable photographs that she will hang on the messy wall of her room, on the headboard of her apartment in Meguro, where I have never been, perhaps she is even carrying a child between her viscera.

I shout: "Where we have never been, Mr. Okuda Crustacean!" In spite of the phone bug, of the monthly payoff to the dancer Kazumi and the cameras installed by the submarine commanded by Mr. Suguro Shibata, professor of the Association of the Harmonious Fugu of Tsukiji.

When I make Mr. Giant Lobster Okuda see that the possibilities are infinite, he, as is to be expected, gets a *big* erection under his kimono.

That's when he starts to destroy Tokyo for real.

Chased by the crowd of adolescents, my father walks in the direction of Ueno, aiming a few kicks at the viaduct where the subway line passes, dragging toppled light posts and electric wires from his sandals. Inside the *patchinko* arcades, thousands of somnambulists in the grip of the machines are awakened by the explosions. Many will die there, staring at metal balls.

When it gets dark, Mr. Lobster Okuda and I will have already stopped counting the dead.

24

The call that beeps at six in the morning on the cell phone of Mr. Suguro Shibata, professor of the Association of the Harmonious Fugu of Tsukiji, is from an old acquaintance who calls him every Tuesday at the same time.

The order from this old acquaintance of Suguro's is, also, always the same: a whole fugu. Not a fugu raised in an aquarium with controlled food and bathed in antibiotics, but a wild fugu. Today, fugu #572 of lot 09.4509.

Fugus can only be eaten after their venomous parts are carefully removed by specialists licensed like Mr. Shibata. The liver, ovaries, and part of the skin of the fugus contain lethal levels of tetrodotoxin, a substance one-thousand-two-hundred times more mortal than cyanide. An average fugu has sufficient venom to kill thirty human beings, thus the extreme care to carefully cut and clean the fish, a process which Mr. Shibata has taught for twenty-three years at the Association of the Harmonious Fugu of Tsukiji.

To the foreign reporters, Mr. Shibata is accustomed to confirming, with undisguised satisfaction, that the first symptom of this poisoning is a numbness on the lips and tongue that manifests itself between twenty minutes and three hours after the ingestion of the *baiacu*. Following this, the tingling spreads to the face and the extremities of the body. Then come headaches, stomach cramps, nausea, and vomiting. The victim has difficulty speaking, walking, and breathing. His skin turns blue and arterial pressure drops. The pupils dilate and muscles contract. The poisoned person becomes totally paralyzed, even though he remains lucid until he dies, which occurs in four to six hours on average. Death will be caused by paralysis of the respiratory muscles.

There is no known antidote for the poison, which led to the prohibition of consumption of fugu during the shogun era of Tokugawa and during the Meiji era. Until today, the fugu is the only food that cannot be on the menu of our emperor, says Suguro. And he continues his memorized text: today, because of the surgical work on the organs like that done by the Association of the Harmonious Fugu of Tsukiji, it's possible to eat the fish with no peril.

All the data that Suguro enumerates makes his work even more important. He never comments on the advances in marine science that conclude that fugu tetrodotoxin come from bacteria ingested by the fish, that when raised in a controlled environment can be one hundred percent safe. Accepting this and the "clean" fugu that come from Utsuki, a city of Oita, would be to recognize that the long and tedious task of cleaning the fugu with precision has its days numbered. And not just that, but the importance and meaning of his own existence, Mr. Suguro Shibata, professor of the Association of the Harmonious Fugu of Tsukiji.

Fortunately, there are still people who understand the importance of a wild fugu, and not by coincidence Mr. Lobster Okuda is one of them. The weekly order is the same as those of the last three decades.

With his work on the fish and all the spy services related to the submarine, Mr. Shibata buys opera discs and takes private voice lessons in lyric opera with a foreign professor who lives in an apartment in Omotesando paid by him. Neither Suguro's wife nor his children know this.

It's funny how subversion starts, thinks Suguro. The money I earn outside the law accompanies the desire that I have to spend it on depraved activities like opera, singing, the young Italian maestro, infinite reenactments of scenes of *Madame Butterfly à deux*. If Mr. Okuda had not corrupted him, Suguro would never have had the courage to involve himself in such activities. The blame, he concludes secretly on his rides in the subway to the apartment in Omotesando, is Mr. Okuda's. The blame belongs to the person who had the idea of going against what is right. And this idea did not come from Suguro.

It's what keeps us together — me, the doll Yoshiko, the dancer Kazumi, and Mr. Suguro Shibata, professor of the Association of the Harmonious Fugu of Tsukiji: we share the same corruptor.

25

I understand very little. For this reason I insist and write these letters: if I don't get the right answers, at least I want to ask good questions.

I can give examples of my lack of comprehension. Certainly they will appear ridiculous and pointless to you, who have been longer in the world than I.

When an electronic switch is turned on and a light comes on, I never understand how the light comes out of the switch that you press with your fingers and then reaches the lamp. The TV is even more incomprehensible, because it doesn't just carry light, but sound, colors, and moving images. I imagine that they must come from somewhere, not very far from here, but how do they get to the device? I feel like a complete idiot, because the human beings of our great nation, accustomed to technology, certainly control these processes and don't sit around asking how the objects turn on and off or how the sound of a voice travels through the air to a phone.

Mr. Okuda taught me in one of his poems the meaning of the word "supernatural," and for me these machines are all supernatural, just like me.

And not just the machines, but human beings are also incomprehensible to me. Every day, I understand less of what is around me. I try to come up with better questions, the right questions, but the answers elude me more and more, as if the questions and answers were inverted magnets that repelled each other.

I did not understand when the foreign woman with the big breasts and blond hair started a few months ago to come to this house and to talk with Mr. Okuda in an unintelligible language during long encounters with the door closed. On those days, my master made me stay inside the box.

At the beginning, that's what I did, but then I started to disobey him. One day I peeked through the slightly open door and saw the foreign woman moving over Mr. Okuda, moving in a way I'd never be capable of, because when I'm with Mr. Okuda, he's the one who moves. I always stay still and quiet. But not the foreign woman. The foreigner moves.

Afterwards Mr. Okuda picked up a few sheets of paper in the marble box on his table, and gave them to Iurana, which is the strange name my master called her. At first, I thought it was money. Then I realized it was nothing like that. Mr. Okuda was giving her manuscripts, but what value would they have to that woman?

My silicone body is one-hundred-thirty centimeters long and weighs twenty-one kilos. I know that the foreign woman weighs almost double and is at least forty centimeters longer than me. Maybe Mr. Atsuo Okuda is after those extra kilos and centimeters, which makes me feel insufficient and inadequate, since my model doesn't come in extra weight or height. If my master has a preference for other measurements, I can't do anything to please him.

There are things that can be perfected and even exchanged in my body, like the hair, the width and depth of my sex, the size and length of my fingers and nails, and even my breasts, the diameter and color of the nipples, but I could never compensate for that difference in height and weight. I can't even say that my disconformity is irretrievable, because I never had anything to retrieve.

Beside this, at what point would a change in my measurements turn me into a different person — since I am my body and my name Yoshiko? How much should I get fatter or grow to stop being who I am and change into another person? What is that boundary?

When I think about Mr. Okuda next to that woman with measurements that are impossible for me to achieve, I feel a focus of precise heat inside my body, as if someone were lighting a match in my chest. I become nervous and incapable of performing my domestic duties, reading, or watching television. The only thought that calms me is to imagine the return of Mr. Okuda to me. But at the next moment, Mr. Okuda doesn't knock on the door, not even at the next minute or the next, and what they call "now" takes a long time to happen, and I feel a great revulsion for everything.

The only way to stop all of this would be to disappear.

And to disappear would mean to be put away in the box where I came from and lose my name Yoshiko, and to remain alone in the dark until I blend with the dark and lose the sense of what is the dark and what is me, and then lose the awareness of my body and with it my body, which is what I am, because I am my body and my name Yoshiko.

But there is a second idea that relieves me and gives me enormous pleasure whenever I cut the poisonous fish for my master. It's to kill Mr. Okuda. And to make the now stop happening to him as well.

26

The men in suits with security ear buds at the door of the Regency
Hyatt of Shinjuku recognize Kazumi, the most lucrative dancer
of the Abracadabar, coveted by the clients, the managers, and by
the clients and managers of the other establishments on the street,
whose private dance or simple company at the table for thirty minutes would cost hundreds of thousands of yen, and they let her go
up as all eyes follow her.

The elevator climbs to the twelfth floor of the hotel, silently, as if
it were not moving.

Kazumi takes a deep breath, runs her fingers through her long
hair, adjusts her leather dress in her reflection, and before she expected, she sees the mirrored doors open, slicing her body into
two equal parts. She exits into the hall with carpeted walls and re-
cessed lighting on the ceiling, walks to the fire escape, and pushes
a metal door that opens with a dry click. After two flights of stairs,
she presses a button on the fire extinguisher that releases a small
aperture in the wall.

The dancer Kazumi kneels down and feels a shiver run down her
back as the door slams behind her. She gropes the dark walls with
her small and very white hands, slides her feet hesitantly along a
sloping tunnel. The place smells of battery fluid. Kazumi descends
what would be half a floor when she is surrounded by an intense
light that closes her eyelids.

The world outside the borders of steel and glass of that skyscraper
seem suddenly irretrievable.

"What are you doing here?"

"I came to see Mr. Atsuo Okuda."

"Mr. Okuda has not informed us of your visit."

"Look, if you don't let me through, you'll have problems."

"What kind of problems?"

"Mr. Okuda needs me."

"You need to tell me what your business is."

"I'm not authorized."

"By who?"

"By Mr. Okuda!"

"Hum."

"And you could be someone he sent to test me."

"I have orders not to let any unidentified person pass."

"That's a lie. This has never happened to me before."

"You know that today the circumstances are different. Haven't you heard about the *disaster*? It's in all the papers. He destroyed entire blocks."

"It doesn't matter. I follow orders."

"Me too."

"So how long are we going to stand around losing time here? And can you take that light out of my face? It's bothering me."

The light blinks three times and diminishes in intensity. Kazumi's pupils take awhile to adapt until they decode the image of her opposing Cerberus. The gatekeeper who stops her from going further is a Cigarette Vending Machine.

"Hey, are you in there?" Kazumi knocks with her splayed hand on the buttons of the machine.

"I *am* the Machine. Don't hurt me."

As the phonemes leave the acrylic panel, the lights that illuminate the multicolored cigarette brands blink in sequence. Kazumi's face and the narrow tunnel are covered in this diffuse light.

"Why am I talking with a Cigarette Vending Machine?"

"I could ask the same question."

"Please let me pass."

"What would you do to get by me?"

"I could unplug you."

"Don't be an idiot. I can be anything. And you know that, Kazumi . . ."

"How do you know my name?"

"You are very famous among us, here in the submarine."

"Why?"

"Among other things, because you have exact geometric proportions. All the triangles that compose your body have dimensions and angles that are Euclidianly exact to the millionth decimal case. What attracts men and women to you are mathematical equations: you are a collection of miraculously harmonious polygons, the only one of the human species with that level of geometrical precision."

"That's ridiculous!"

"No, it's not. You know you are not exactly beautiful. Or no more so than your workmates at the club. Even so you are a success. This is because men need geometry, even though they don't know it."

"You're crazy."

"You are an aberration among human beings, the only perfectly proportioned woman on the planet, talking with a Cigarette Vending Machine. How do you feel about finding out that everything you are is summed up in a bunch of measurements? You are your body, nothing else."

"Shut up!"

"I can tell you the date when you will die. Do you want to know?"

"Of course not."

"And if I told you the day and month?"

The piercing sound of a microphone interrupts the conversation and gives space to the voice of Mr. Okuda that echoes through the corridor. My father says that the Machine may let Kazumi pass. Without questioning the order of Mr. Okuda, the Cigarette Vending Machine moves away from the field of vision of our periscope carried by its little metal wheels to a lateral pantographic door. The dancer Kazumi is now in the dark again and just needs to take two steps before entering room 1212, occupied by Mr. Okuda.

"How are you able to go through there? Even I have to bend over . . ."

"After yesterday's disaster, I don't need to go that way anymore."

Mr. Okuda remains static in the shadows. The dancer Kazumi, like us, can't see anything outside the cone of light that starts on the surface of the table and ends in the interior of a metal cupola hanging from the ceiling. This includes a black telephone, the arms, legs, the kimono, trunk, and practically the entire body of Mr. Okuda, with the exception of his right hand, that now lifts the hand-rolled cigarette to the ashtray, that, like Kazumi, we can't see. No light enters through the window or the crack at the bottom of the door.

The smoke produced by the hand-rolled cigarette runs through the cone of opaque air. What holds the cigarette, before extinguishing it in the ashtray we can't see, is Mr. Okuda's right hand.

"Where is the foreign woman?"

"Mr. Okuda, I assure you that the gaijin has Shunsuke in the palm of her hand. Your son is madly in love with her. And she is with me. Or rather . . . It's just a question of time until Iulana Romiszowska convinces Shunsuke. Then our control will be complete."

"Your speech is so perfect that I don't trust you. You had promised me progress weeks ago. Now the girl disappears in Akihabara."

"But sir, I'm telling you the truth. You'll soon have Shunsuke back at home, with you and the doll Yoshiko Okuda. And Iulana Romiszowska too."

"I don't like you to call Mrs. Okuda a doll."

"Sorry, sir!"

"Kazumi, your presence here gives me a high degree of excitement. I cannot remain calm."

"I can do as you wish, sir. The ropes . . .?"

"Stop this nonsense, Kazumi. I know that Iulana Romiszowska has not tried to contact you since she disappeared."

" . . . "

"Do you have any leads on where the foreign woman is?"

" . . . "

"Do you remember that dream that Iulana told you?"

" . . . "

"I know you are covering up for the Russian. You think I'm an idiot like my son? It's going to be today, Kazumi."

"Please, no!"

"And it's going to be filmed by the submarine. You know that, after what happened, I will not be able to leave this room for some time. But even so, I will be able to hear and see everything, Kazumi."

"The ropes, sir . . ."

My father ignores Kazumi's pleas. Mr. Lobster Okuda dials a sequence of numbers on the black telephone outside the cone of light that projects over the square table behind the locked door of room 1212 of the Shinjuki Hyatt Regency, and calls Mr. Suguro Shibata, professor of the Association of the Harmonious Fugu of Tsukiji.

"The boys, Suguro."

27

When the focus of the lens converges to the center of the mat, we see Mr. Suguro, professor of the Association of the Harmonious Fugu of Tsukiji, sitting on a small bench, his erect back at a right angle to the plank of polished wood. His torso is illuminated by the afternoon that traces diagonal patterns on the kimono and the recently painted walls. Next to him is the foreign professor who gives him voice lessons in the secret apartment. The Italian, before sitting on the floor of the bachelor's pad in Omotesando, invites the group in.

The Italian recruited them on the street, but Mr. Shibata will be the one responsible for the selection of the boys. Of the thirty-two who now lounge around the wooden bench, only eight will be chosen. In exchange for a wad of bank notes that Mr. Shibata will take out of his metal briefcase, they will be responsible for reenacting on Kazumi the dream of Iulana Romiszowska.

While the adolescents organize themselves in a circle around the two, the foreigner whispers in English into Mr. Shibata's ear:

"I don't understand the meaning of this."

"Understand? You don't need to understand."

"You've never questioned these orders?"

"No."

"Why?"

"Don't you have a patron who supports you? Well I do too, and I have to do what Mr. Okuda commands. And I'd do the same if he didn't pay me anything."

For the first time Mr. Shibata raises the tone of his voice at the young teacher.

Mr. Shibata claps his hands to quiet the buzz filling the space of the room. The young men straighten their shoulders and grow silent in unison. The professor of the Association of the Harmonious Fugu of Tsukiji grasps his fine mustache with his index finger and thumb and smoothes it to either side of his face, rests his closed right hand on his waist, and orders that all the boys, invisible adolescents of the middle class, dressed in hoodies and high tops, take down their pants.

The silence in the room reaches another tone; a few of the boys exchange glances. Mr. Shibata again claps his hands:

"Let's get going, you louts! I don't have time for this! You want the money?"

When all of them have their pants and briefs at their knees, Mr. Shibata breathes deeply, moves his face closer, closes his eyes, and begins to inspect them.

28

You, Kazumi, leave work and go home, stepping forcefully on the sidewalk. It is night and the noise of your boots on the stone enlarges your presence on the dark street. You always liked occupying a space bigger than yourself and, as a dancer and escort, you know the artifices for doing this.

Above your route is a viaduct, and now the last train is passing over it. You, guided by the moonlight and the shadows of the lampposts, rehearse your lines to the emptiness for a few kilometers until, in the passageway to the Hanazono temple, a dark corridor with wooden doors and red lanterns, you see a group of young men gathered around a garbage fire. They are adolescents of the lower middle class, dressed in hoodies and high top sneakers. As you go by, you notice they are not looking at you.

It's as if you were invisible to them, Kazumi.

A few meters ahead, you feel a whack on your shoulders that propels your body ahead in a rapid trajectory until your face lands in a puddle of water on the sidewalk. You think: my clothes got dirty. Then you think: how did I fall? Opening your eyes, you see half a dozen pairs of shoes. You think of asking for help to get up, but you hear a muffled sound. You hug your body. After the first blows, you can't distinguish the origin of each of the foci of pain.

If you protect your face with your hands, you'll leave the rest of your body vulnerable, and vice versa. You think of giving up. After minutes (or hours, you wouldn't know), you think: I want to go to sleep so it will stop. I want to die so it will stop. It will not stop, Kazumi.

You are lifted to your feet by your hair and your clothing, dragged along the ground like a puppet. The men tear your clothes with sharpened nails. They uncover your breasts and the first thing you think is: I am beautiful.

They agree and advance on you like starving calves, biting and tearing your pink nipples with their canines, your throat exposed. You are licked by all of these little street urchins, younger than you, invisible during the day, perhaps they are teenagers, and you feel a disassociated relief: as strong as the sucking on your body, it is weaker than the toes of their shoes on your nipples. You think of reacting and escaping, but your feet don't touch the ground, your arms only flail in the air. You are an imprisoned dove inside a mirrored room, being hurled against the walls.

Now you hear a siren and you open your eyes with difficulty, enough to see a band of blue light twirling through the buildings, columns, and stone dragons that open the way to the Hanazono temple. You see a police car approach slowly. You try to scream but you can't. The hands imprisoning your body drop it on the ground: the shouts of the men and the alarm become mute. The police stop the car and look at you. They smile, Kazumi.

The tires of the police car give a sharp squeal and carry the car, its siren, and the blue light far from there.

The arms that imprison you gain new strength and again pull your feet off the ground. Now you are carried by a big garbage bin. You feel your cold feet and think: I've lost my shoes. You feel your naked legs and think: my skirt. You feel a shiver between your legs.

The men are dry but not more than you. The path is difficult, and in the beginning, irritated by the difficulty, they hit your face. You don't feel anything, but you hear the sharp sound of the slaps, louder than the incomprehensible moans, mixed phonemes, consonants in collision. One of them holds your arms behind your back, while two others grab your legs that shake in pallid tremors. While one advances ahead, the other boys in rapid gestures drop their pants (you hear the buzz of zippers) and they rub hunks of hot flesh on your face, wetting your skin with a mixture of sweats. You try to identify the origins of the smells and tastes and think: the youngest one is sweet, the fat one is salty. They are all bitter.

You are turned over and now they advance on your back. Your

face streams liquid from your nose, gums, and eyebrows: a red puddle forms on the ground, dry branches from an ochre tree pressed into the stones on the path to the temple. From time to time you feel waves of heat running between your legs, your breasts, in your eyes — gluing your eyelashes together and clouding your vision even more.

You think, I must be dead. Because they manipulate you, Kazumi, the way you cut, guard, and touch a cadaver, the way you undress and dress the exposed body of a dead person. You feel as if they are hanging your entrails on hooks for exhibition, to be analyzed by curious childlike hands, as if you were present along with the living at your own necropsy on the monitors of the Periscope Room or even on a movie screen showing hallways full of the viscera of your dead body.

But you are not dead. You don't have permission, Kazumi.

And then you feel vertigo at a central point of your guts, and you let yourself fall like a child. That's when you start to like being there.

29

A large amount of time went by outside of this apartment since I have locked myself in here.

To return to *taking action* would be like watering the ocean with a medicine dropper. Even so, in the last few weeks I have felt a strange presence, like the vibration of a TV off the air behind a half-open door.

I am not a *hikikomori*, one of those vagrants supported by their relatives who are awakened every eight hours with banging on the door and a plate of food on the floor. I am really alone, and very dead. The others are also already dead, imprisoned in the future in photos at the bottom of some drawer or in a file in a broken computer.

Our difference is that *I* already know this.

After the disappearance of the foreign woman and the solution that he found for Kazumi, my father stopped looking for me. He locked himself in his house (a familiar habit), accompanied by the doll Yoshiko. I imagine that the venerable Mr. Okuda has not died yet, or the newspapers would have already knocked at my door to get an obituary that already must have been written twenty years ago.

I think of all of this, after so much time, because the phone is ringing now, and continues to ring, and now again, and every ring reminds me that there is another time zone outside the frontiers of this apartment.

"Shun?"

The voice of Iulana Romiszowska grates in my head. Before I can articulate a way of saying that her survival offends me, Iulana begins to tell me that the dancer Kazumi has just died, after months on life-support machines, and that the police didn't want to give any information and practically kicked her out of the police station. She asked if I didn't read the news of the beating in the papers.

I say I haven't read anything in a long time, and I grow silent.

"I called because I need your help."

"Why?"

"When I looked through Kazumi's things at the apartment, I found a number of short notes, all written on the same letter stock. She received those papers the night she was assaulted. You know who I'm talking about, right?"

" . . ."

"She also received a lot of calls from Mr. Okuda in the early hours of the morning. I think he paid her to spy on us."

"Why haven't you brought this to the police?"

"They said if I bothered them again they would deport me. I'm illegal. And afraid, because the phone is ringing in the middle of the night again."

"Do you answer it?"

"Yes. And your father says just one thing."

"What?"

"Where is your question? I am an answer waiting for your question."

"What an old shit."

"And then I hang up, because I can't say anything. I just don't want it to happen to me, Shun."

We made a date to meet at the cheap imitation of Dunkin' Donuts near the Shinjuku station. The effect of leaving the house after so long is curious: I am an explorer. My legs and eyes hurt, the roads all look the same, even though they lead to the same place. The human beings on these streets truly disgust me: they are dirty, ugly, incapable, greedy, gross, and miserly. To avoid contact with my fellow human beings, I wear gloves and an anti-pollen mask. Ergo my scuba outfit, and in it I navigate through the filthy waters now forgotten by the submarine.

The foreign woman seems as faded as the light of the buildings and the color of the other human beings. I don't recognize the clothes she is wearing, they look new, but I still recognize the angular shape of her breasts, the clear halo of her nipples, the whiteness of her neck where her hair starts, an expression of astonishment, a smile, a way of spreading out her body when she sleeps, the timbre of her nocturnal voice calling my name. Even so, I think I have lost something fundamental and unspeakable about this new woman. Something makes her a total stranger sitting at my table.

She orders a croissant and a double espresso. She swallows it without manners, like a famished animal. The only customers, besides us, are a Chinese family. I have the strange impression of seeing myself from the outside, in a picture, sitting with a foreign woman. Outside the picture it is eleven at night on a Sunday and the café is half-empty. The attendants are different. The old ones, who knew us and silently rooted for me during the long hours of waiting, must have gotten better jobs or, with luck, left Tokyo — the world went on in our absence. Another thing we have in common with the dead.

Before I give in to the temptation to ask what the Polish-Romanian has been doing the past few months, and with whom, she puts the notes on the table. I don't need to read anything to know that they are from my father. I am not impressed by the irresponsibility of the old man in sending correspondence on personal letterhead to the dancer Kazumi, who he would make disappear with the staging of a rape.

"Shun, what do I do with this? If you don't help me, I'm going to give it to the men in the club today."

30

At the appointed hour, Iulana and I take the subway under the slanted stares of the crowd — they imagine that Iulana is one of those Russian models who end up as whores in Japan, and I am a salaryman with exotic taste. We enter the sixth car and take a seat, under a little crepe marking on the ceiling. In front of us, an adolescent concentrates intensely on texting something on a cell phone. Across from us, an elderly couple plays double Sudoku. The LCD monitors advertise products, the next stations, the weather conditions.

The train stops.

The landscape we see through the window stops being a blur of horizontal streaks to freeze into shapes backlit by the rain. Next to the bridge where the Yamamoto line runs, there is a wall of buildings and commercial galleries. On top of everything, a big billboard advertises soup in neon lights. The only set of windows without closed curtains or darkened glass is on the fifth floor of the curved building at the right. There, a group of little ballerinas rehearses a dance in the middle of the room, while others stretch their legs on a metal barre. The movement of the girls is so *pure* that I think of tapping you on the shoulder and sharing the ballerinas with you.

But this will never happen, because the work of Mr. Suguro Shibata, professor of the Association of the Harmonious Fugu of Tsukiji, and of his pupils, will go as planned. And the reach of my hand to your body will be interrupted by the explosion.

The boom starts with a high-pitched sound at the front of the car that runs through us like a sharp katana saber. As the impact advances through the seats and the human beings in them, the groaning of twisted metal takes on a serious tone. The alteration is sudden: where before there was a sense of continuity and order, now there is entropy. The first to be taken by the shock wave is the adolescent who is texting something on a cell phone. Next to him a gray blister in the door that connects the cars swells and gains momentum, like a fish taking in air and then exploding, exposing sharpened claws that take the kid by the torso, perforating his body. In a rapid pitching motion, the metal teeth lift him to the ceiling. The boy's blood squirts onto the faces of the old people sitting in the front. Before they have time to react, they are swallowed by a solid wall that takes the left side of the car.

In the midst of the metallic groans of the explosion, I hear a loud laugh and a phlegmy cough. It's Mr. Lobster Okuda, who observes us with a satisfied expression behind the monitors of the Periscope Room.

The jelly of human remains, pieces of iron and plastic registered by the cameras, advances slowly, taking on other bodies and objects, in a leaden cyclone with red fringes. The metallic groaning joins the sound of skulls cracking.

They're like ripe grapes, Iulana.

The floor of the car twists, its ceiling is transformed into a sheer precipice. And now we are the ones who take flight, suspended over the ground, in the grip of a wave about to break. The armrests sway as if they were in an earthquake, the LCD monitors flicker erratically before being sucked into the vortex of destruction.

Things are happening. Now, Iulana.

Soon we will hear nothing more. There will be just silence and cold when the chaos takes over half the train car. The wave is almost on us. The "accident" as they will call what is happening here. I feel superior, I can say, because *they* will never know the motives of this orchestrated event. *They*, who at this moment are entering and leaving Tokyo in well-lit trains and who are ingested, processed, and expelled every day through the guts of this animal of concrete and electricity. *They*, who are completely unaware of what is happening here while they enter elevators, sidewalks, tunnels, escalators, moving walkways, platforms, the long subterranean tunnels of the stations, who won't interrupt their perpetual movement for our small tragedy. *They*, who perhaps in a few hours may find out about our story, the "accident" they will call what is happening now, and they will be moved and fearful seeing our news at the kitchen table while they eat breakfast early in the morning — and I confess that "tomorrow" already seems like a word and a concept that is totally absurd. *They*, who will think about death for a brief instant to later forget the matter and return to the streets and to their trains, as if we were not waiting for them at some fixed point in the future. *They*, who will never be able to understand everything that is happening here, because there is something in this train car that is inimitable and sublime.

Even so, they will try to move the story forward. I imagine the newspaper headlines, maybe the picture of Iulana's remains tossed on the tracks. Very little will be left, they will have to take DNA tests from little pieces of charred flesh and bone. I imagine them poking around your corpse, like those crime scene investigators, and I think that I'd be useless at forensic medicine — I am even thankful for the miserable job I've had the last few years.

And I think of you, Iulana Romiszowska, your thick fingers and solid calves, and the long way that all the parts of your body traveled from Poland to your childhood in the port city of Constanţa, on the edge of the Black Sea, in Romania, until your big, round, blue eyes found the illuminated monster of Tokyo, and not without some amazement, you found me — and at this moment I just wish you could also think about me, who knows how.

I feel a strange sense of peace, Iulana.

It's as if I were submerged under the surface of something new. I know that I'm almost not here, and that brings me a sense of immediate nostalgia, as if I were reconstructing a dream, waking in the middle of a long déjà vu at the same time that the misshapen chaos of steel and ground meat silently gallops in our direction. The darkness takes over everything, as if taking back something that always belonged to it.

It's all very natural, Iulana.

We observe this wave with calm indifference, in spite of the certainty of nearing the end, or because of it.

When you finally turn to me, our eyes meet in an empty place. And before I have time to tap you on the shoulder to share the ballerinas dancing in white dresses on the fifth floor of the curved building to the right, under the big billboard that is advertising soup in neon lights, silhouettes backlit by the rain, before the silence takes over your eyes, you'll still have time to say my name, for the last time you'll say my name, Iulana Romiszowska, for the last time you'll say my name with your nocturnal voice.

31

The raindrops splatter on the roof and on the carpet of dead flowers on the ground. The crows seek shelter under the arc of the naked cherry trees. At the entrance to the garden, Mr. Lobster Okuda and I observe in silence the outline of the cremated corpse of Iulana Romiszowska, retrieved from the scene of the accident last year by Mr. Suguro Shibata, professor of the Association of the Harmonious Fugu of Tsukiji.

"That burned grass will take a while to get color again," my father says as if he were talking about the weather. And he grumbles that after the explosion, Mr. Shibata resigned, and now he doesn't have anyone to take care of the submarine or the garden. "It's true you're back. But now besides being a leech you're a cripple."

Mr. Okuda Crustacean looks me over with his buggy eyes — after nine months in the hospital, the half of my body that still works balances on a wheel chair. My father grunts at me, which means I should come in. It will be the first time in fourteen years that I cross this threshold.

"Today the person who will prepare the welcome fugu is Yoshiko. You will enjoy meeting her," he says.

TRANSLATOR'S AFTERWORD
Translating the "nocturnal Voices" of J. P. Cuenca's Twenty-first Century Tokyo

Ilan Stavans has noted that "modernity . . . is not lived through nationality but . . . through translationality."[1] Just as translation is a border-crossing activity, the writing coming from the contemporary new writers of Latin America is transnational in nature, illuminating both the experience of cultural otherness and epistemological otherness derived from their experiences as global travelers and citizens. J. P. Cuenca is in the vanguard of Brazilian writing in this genre. The only cultural reference to Brazil in *The Only Happy Ending for a Love Story Is an Accident*, is the briefest mention of the singer João Gilberto, whose "nocturnal voice" becomes a refrain in the narrative. This is not what readers would expect of a young writer born in Rio de Janeiro, but interestingly it is his bestselling book both inside and out of Brazil. J. P. Cuenca began work on this book while living in Tokyo in 2007 and continued to immerse himself in research on Japan in the three following years while traveling elsewhere in the world. He chose Tokyo because of a lifelong fascination with Japanese culture and the aptness of the setting to the type of futuristic entropy that he wished to convey. The choice of setting also originated from childhood experiences watching Japanese animated series (the monster Gyodai is from the Japanese television series Dengeki Sentai Changeman), and from the emotional impact on him of the events of September 2011 with the destruction of the Twin Towers, among other influences. The action takes place in 2013, in a not too distant future from the date of publication (2010). The story is told by a silicone doll (Yoshiko) and a Japanese salaryman (Shunsuke), son of a mad poet Atsuo Okuda. These two voices rise out of the cacophony of Tokyo, which the author describes as "waking to a nightmare," a city almost as impossible to portray as it is to photograph, with its dizzying panorama of light, sound, and rapidly moving images. In an interview about the "visual education" that the Japanese have, Cuenca suggests that westerners lack an ability to process the bombardment on the senses that Tokyo produces on foreigners: "My first sensation was disorientation and (entering) a dreamlike state. And of experiencing fiction. That there I was walking through a borderland."

Rendering this novel into English from Brazilian Portuguese requires retracing those steps through the borderland and pressing the narrative through various filters. Cuenca performs a ventriloquist's trick on the voices of Shunsuke and Yoshiko in a way that makes them both sound surreal and mechanical, like robots that appear in other parts of the book. Indeed both characters are the creations of the mad poet, prisoners (albeit willing) of his schemes to control them and those with whom they come into contact. There is also the otherworldly nature of the tale, with its recounting of elaborate dreams (as told by Shunsuke's love interest, the Romanian waitress Iulana, to her roommate and lover Kazumi and by Shunsuke to Iulana) as well as the ghoulish description of the "accident" that begins the novel and is repeated, with the most subtle of variations, in four different places in the text. The poetic rants of Mr. Atsuo Okuda, whose apparition pursues his son at the most inopportune times, add to the atmosphere of the insane asylum. In one scene, the exotic dancer Kazumi has a surreal conversation with a cigarette vending machine that is blocking her access to her paymaster, the mad poet.

So how does Cuenca's translator bridge borders in this adventure in "translationality?" Gregory Rabassa tells of his apprehension over translating the young Colombian writer Jorge Franco in his marvelous memoir, *Translation and Its Dyscontents*: "When I first got *Rosario Tijeras* I wondered if I would be up to and adequate for the translation of a book from the new generation."[2] He evidently found his stride in the translation and discovered "he wasn't all that distant from the story," given his deep familiarity with the "Latin American tale." He also discovered that the age difference was no bar to the translation of a contemporary work. He reflects, "in fact it might well be that a set of older eyes might see things in a more universal light and thus extract the permanence of the text better. Had I been a different age I might have used that horrid verb 'to universalize' above and not thought of it, Joyce-wise, as universal eyes."[3] There is much to connect translator and writer in the recreation of this unique tale. While the voice is highly original and a product of a bright young Brazilian intellectual who is at home in the capitals of the world, there are also deeply imbedded cultural experiences that come through in the language and the manner of telling the tale. A self-professed admirer of the great Brazilian detective writer Rubem Fonseca, whom J. P. Cuenca claims to have read as a precocious nine-year old boy, there are unmistakable traces of Fonseca's syntax, manner of rendering dialogue, and penchant for the sexual taboo in the narrative (for example, the doll Yoshiko conjures up the love doll in Fonseca's classic story "Stuff of a Dream"). The cadences of the narrative, while they reflect oneiric madness of the setting, pay homage to the lyrical voice of João Gilberto. The translation challenges were mitigated by the fact that Cuenca's language is simple and direct, not needful of the ephemeral slang of current international pop culture. It is precisely Cuenca's "translationality" that makes the task of his translator significant and encourages carrying his text across to English speaking readers in ways that Bermann and Wood suggest might urge this new audience to rethink globalization in more carefully defined, more humanistic terms.[4]

Elizabeth Lowe

NOTES

1. Neal Sokol, "Translation and Its Discontents: A Conversation with Ilan Stavans," *The Literary Review*, 45 (2002): 554.

2. Gregory Rabassa, *If This Be Treason: Translation and its Dyscontents, A Memoir* (New York: New Directions, 2005), 175.

3. Rabassa, *If This Be Treason*, 177.

4. Sandra Bermann and Michael Wood, Nation, *Language, and the Ethics of Translation* (Princeton: Princeton University Press, 2005).